A Walk to the Hills of the Dreamtime

Also by James Vance Marshall

WALKABOUT
A RIVER RAN OUT OF EDEN
MY BOY JOHN THAT WENT TO SEA

a walk
to the hills
of the
dreamtime

by James Vance Marshall

Illustrations by Lydia Rosier

William Morrow and Company, Inc.
New York 1970

A glossary of Aborigine, plant and animal names appears on pages 141–149.

Printed in the United States of America.
Library of Congress Catalog Card Number 79-96301

The Australian Aboriginal does not transplant. His altars are waterholes, hills and rocks. He is, by the nature of his beliefs, identified with and bound to a particular patch of earth, his tribal land. That land, and no other, is identified with his "dreaming."

COLIN SIMPSON: *Adam in Ochre*

A Walk to the Hills of the Dreamtime

Chapter 1

It was midday; the outback lay drugged to immobility by the heat of the sun, and the only moving thing was the Landrover churning in a cocoon of dust along the fair-weather track between Alice Springs and The Granites. In the driver's seat the stockman was on the alert, watching for dust devils and the drifts of fine-as-talcum-powder mud. In the back the children were asleep.

They lay sprawled out among the crates of provisions: brother and sister, oblivious to the heat of the sun. The little Aboriginal boy slept soundly; but the girl was restless, dreaming.

She dreamed that she was standing again (as she had stood only a couple of days ago) in the panelled hall of the Melville Island mission, holding her brother very tight by the hand and listening to the voice of the Mother Superior. "It's a wonderful chance, Sarah," the voice was saying, "both for you and for Joey. And you'll be able to stay together."

"Yes, ma'am," she said.

"Tableland is one of the biggest stations in the Territory. Mr. and Mrs. Grantly are fine Christian people. And I'm sure you'll be happy there."

"Yes, ma'am," she said.

"It's a shock, I know. And a rush. But Mrs. Grantly wants you right away, before the wet, and there's a truck coming to pick you up this afternoon. Now before you get ready, my dears, is there anything—anything at all—that you'd like to ask?"

Silence, her brother shifting from foot to foot, and a voice that she hardly recognized as her own: "Our mother. Suppose she comes back from the sea. How'll she find us?"

"My dear,"—the missionary's voice was gentle—"if your mother ever comes back we'll send for you. I promise."

The dream grew blurred. And the one thing that stood out clearly from the whirlwind of packing and good-byes was her teacher's last-minute plea—"And Sarah! See Joey remembers his prayers." Then they were waving back to the long, low, sprawling huts of the mission which had been their home for the last half dozen years,

and the truck was heading for Tableland *via* Alice Springs. To start with, the children had been a little in awe of the stockman who was driving because he was big and white and needed a shave and smelled of beer; but after a while his kindness got through to them. Soon they were taking it in turn to ride up front, and the stockman was feeding them sticks of barley sugar and telling them of the great grey mobs of cattle that drifted over the station plains and the fifty-odd bores that were needed to bring them water and the thousand-odd horses that were needed to keep the mob on the move in a never-ending battle with undernourishment and drought. And by the end of the first day they were friends.

It was eight hundred miles from Melville Island to Alice Springs; eight hundred miles of dusty grind through a tired red landscape old as time. The children loved it: the spiky clumps of spinifex, the pallid smoothly sculptured gums, the tribal smoke rings rising blue over the limestone bluffs, and the stockman's apparently inexhaustible capacity for Cooper beer. It was all exciting and new. But in The Alice there took place an incident that the girl would have liked to forget.

It was early morning. They had just finished loading crates of provisions into the truck, and she was standing in the shade of the store's verandah studying a map of the Macdonnell Ranges, very conscious of the fact that the storekeeper was studying her. She knew by the blood that was in her what was coming.

"Hey you!"

She turned unwillingly.

"How many years you have, eh?"

"I'm fourteen," she said. She could read his mind like a book.

"Hmmm! Your father: he a rubbish-one white?"

"My father," she said between her teeth, "was a Japanese pearl diver."

The storekeeper nodded. That, he told himself, would account for her slim waist, her delicate features and the unusual fineness of her skin and hair. "Hey, Al!" He turned to the stockman who had just finished checking the provisions. "I go for your bit o' black velvet!"

The stockman's voice was without rancour: "Shut your mouth, you old bastard. She's a mission kid I'm taking back as Mrs. Grantly's maid."

The storekeeper was unabashed. He patted Sarah's behind. "Lucky Mrs. Grantly!" He peered at the sky in the north, noting the herringbone patterns of cirrus. "You'd best be on your way if you want to git back before the wet. An' watch for cock-eyed Bobs*—or you and Black Velvet'll be taking a roll in the desert!"

A revving up of the engine, a waving of hands, and they were setting out on the final stage of the journey to Tableland.

The girl sat very still, her eyes on the spinifex, her lips pressed tightly together. A more sensitive man would have realized the way she felt; would have offered her

---

* A *cock-eyed Bob* or *willy-willy* is the Australian name for a dust devil: the spinning column of air which often forms in the heat of the day when a breeze is blowing over the blazing desert.

4

the reassurance that there weren't many whites of the storekeeper's kind in the world to which she was being taken. But sensitivity wasn't the stockman's forte. He whistled "Morning Town Ride" and opened a blue-capped Cooper, and all he thought of offering the girl was a stick of barley sugar.

It was midday; the temperature was 108 degrees Fahrenheit, and in the back of the truck the children slept.

They were halfway now between Alice Springs and The Granites, in the center of the Macdonnell Ranges, one of the loneliest deserts on earth; mile after hundred square mile of laterite escarpment, waterless plain and salt-pan depression: not a good place to be lost in. Several times the stockman was tempted to pull up for a siesta; but he knew that as soon as the rains broke the road would be transformed within hours to a sea of mud; so he drove on through the midday heat, watching the track and the cock-eyed Bobs which were stalking the desert like waterspouts the sea. Every now and then he glanced at the sky to the north. The cirrus was still there; but of the expected rain clouds there was no sign.

After a while they came to a gully which the road followed down through a rift in the plateau, twisting and turning this way and that between grotesquely riven blocks of granite—gargantuan playbricks scattered in random drifts along the bed of what had once been a river.

It happened without warning.

One second they were skirting a boulder half the size of a cathedral: the next the cock-eyed Bob was on them.

It came swirling round a bend in the gully, hidden from sight till the moment it struck them: a three-hundred-foot column of viciously spinning air. It hit the truck side on, knocked it into a skid, and smashed it against an outcrop of granite.

The stockman was flung sideways. He was shouting a warning when a knife-edged ledge of rock burst through the windshield and caught him flush on the base of the neck. A pyramid of fire tore through his brain. For a second he was blind with agony. Then in a great white flood came a stillness more absolute than any other he had ever known.

The cock-eyed Bob whirled playfully up the gully. The truck lay on its side, its wheels spinning slowly to a halt. The dust settled. And everything was very quiet.

Chapter 2

Silence; then a splintering crash as a crate in the back of
the Landrover was levered aside. "Joey!" The girl's
voice was frightened. "You all right?"

The boy (as is often the way with eleven-year-olds)
was very matter-of-fact. "Yeah. But I'm under a crate.
An' I can't move."

She eased one of the big wooden boxes of provisions,
as gently as she could, away from his legs. "Can you
wriggle your toes?"

"I'm all right. Don't fuss." He crawled blinking out of
the chaos of piled-up crates like a goanna out of its hide.

She helped him over the side of the truck, and, more shaken than hurt, they stood staring at the wreckage. And the stockman. He was sprawled half in and half out of the driver's seat, his eyes astare at the sun.

"Oh poor Al!" The girl cradled his face in her hands. She thought for a moment that he was simply concussed; then she became aware of the blood seeping out of the side of his mouth and the peculiar angle of his head. Her eyes opened wide. "Get some water. Quick."

But by the time the boy had unearthed the carrier and a beaker, she realized that Al Lowson was beyond the need of water. Her fingers moved to her crucifix. "Joey," she whispered. "He's dead."

They sat on a ledge of granite, watching and waiting, while heat drained slowly out of the sky and the rocks turned, chameleonlike, from red to gold. The girl had decided, very sensibly, to stay by the wreck of the truck. Another car, she told herself, was bound to pass them sooner or later, maybe today, maybe tomorrow; in the meanwhile they had shade and plenty of food and water. Every so often she steeled herself to kneel by the body of the stockman, listening without hope for a flutter of heartbeat; only when Al Lowson's body began to stiffen did she make the sign of the cross on his forehead and close his eyes.

The sun slid under the rim of the gully; the sky turned applemint-green; a sunset breeze swirled up the dust, and in the brief subtropic twilight the girl shivered. "Looks like we're here for the night."

"We'll want a fire, then?" The boy was very self-possessed.

She nodded; she doubted if they'd need the warmth, but it would be as well to have something to do. They found a stratum of sandstone, cleared a patch about four feet square, and with sharp-edged flints scooped out a shallow trough. Then they looked round for wood. There wasn't much, but about fifty yards down the gully they discovered a cluster of yacca. They wrenched out the oldest of the eight-foot sapless stems, and fossicked among the roots for resin. They weren't very expert; Aboriginal children brought up in the desert would have collected twice as much in half the time; but eventually they got the yacca-wood snapped into burnable lengths and the resin ground into powder. "Can you make a spark, Joey?"

"I *think* I could. But let's use the stockman's lighter."

An hour later the fire was blazing bright as a lightship adrift in the midnight sea. The children sat close to it, spreading their hands to its warmth and listening to the muted sounds of the outback: the flip-flap-flip of the flying foxes, the long sad wail of the pardalote, and the patter of flying ants mating in midair, shedding their wings and falling intertwined to the rocks. They weren't exactly frightened; but it was a far cry from the dormitories of the Melville Island mission.

After a while the boy began to fidget. "Sarah!"

"Hmmm?"

"This Tableland place we're going to. What's it like?"

"I don't know, Joey. But Mother Superior said we'd like it."

"How does *she* know?"

She traced a pattern in the sand with a stump of yacca. "I reckon it'll be O.K."

Silence, and the stars aglow like pinheads of acetylene.

The boy stirred up the fire. "You remember those smoke rings, the ones we saw on the way to The Alice?"

"Hmmm!"

"You reckon they was made by Mummy's people?"

She shook her head. "Mummy's people live in the Kimberleys, way up north."

A longer silence this time. Then, suddenly eager: "Couldn't we walk to the Kimberleys?"

"Oh Joey! It's *much* too far. Remember what happened to that Mr. Burke and Wills."

"They was know-nothing whites. I bet *we* wouldn't get lost."

She started to unplait her hair. "Forget it. It's time for bed. And nobody's walking anywhere."

She spoke, she hoped, with conviction. But it disturbed her to know that her brother's thoughts had been running so closely parallel to hers.

They banked up the fire with discs of laterite and ash, and smoothed out an area of sandstone on which to doss down. Then it occurred to the girl that they ought perhaps to be showing a light in case a search party came to look for them. She peered at the dashboard of the truck. "You know how to put the lights on?"

"Sure. That big switch by the steering wheel."

After a good deal of poking and prodding and pulling of wrong knobs, a solitary beam flickered palely out of one of the sidelights.

They settled down together, close to the fire. The sandstone was knobbly; but they were shocked and tired and it wasn't long before their breathing grew slower and deeper. After a while, half awake, half asleep, the girl reached for her brother's hand. Normally he'd have snatched it away. But he didn't now. He snuggled close to her. A veil of cirrus came drifting over the moon. A pair of marsupial rats, their eyes aglow like luminous peas, hopped fossicking over the crates. And the children slept.

She could hear the grinding together of her teeth. She was half aware that she was dreaming, but this didn't make her terror any less real. She was in the center of a big and brightly lit room; it wasn't a room that she had ever been in before, but she was convinced (in the inconsequential way one has of being sure of things in dreams) that it was the stockmen's quarters in Tableland. And a man was staring at her; a man she recognized: the storekeeper from Alice Springs. She turned, and there he was again on the opposite side of the room barring her escape: paunchy, white, unshaved and smelling of rum, his sharp little eyes stripping the clothes from her body. She blundered about the room this way and that, like a panic-stricken bird at the bars of its cage. And everywhere she turned the storekeeper was blocking her way. He didn't touch her. He only stared. And stared and

stared, a little dribble of saliva drooling wet out of the corner of his mouth. The lights in the room went out, and she woke, trembling and damp with sweat.

The stars were fading, a belt of cumulus had blotted out the moon, and the sidelight of the truck, its battery exhausted, stared blankly into the night. She squeezed her brother's hand so tightly that he grunted, half woke and rolled impatiently away from her. She lay on her back, staring at the stars; they looked cold, uncomforting and very far away, and it was a long time before she dared to let herself drift back to sleep.

She woke in the pale half-light of dawn and reached automatically for her brother.

He wasn't there.

She scrambled to her feet, fear welling up in her like blood from a cut. For a terrifying moment she thought that he must have set off by himself to walk to the Kimberleys. Then she saw him. He was a dozen yards from the fire, standing on one leg and staring out across the desert to the distant mountains of the north. In the uncertain light he looked taller and older.

"Joey! What are you doing?"

He didn't move.

She went up to him and spoke again—"Hey, Joey!" —but he went on staring straight in front of him as if in a trance. She took his arm and began to lead him back to the fire. At first he moved with the careful precision of a sleepwalker; then he started to shiver. She lowered him to the sandstone and cradled his head in her lap and ran her hands gently over his forehead, and after a while

his shivering stopped and he lay very still. "What were you thinking of?"

He said that he didn't know.

How *could* he know? How could he be expected to put into words the compulsions of a way of life that was already old when Cheops began to build his pyramid? For twenty thousand years his ancestors had lived and died, unchanging, among the secret waterholes of the Australian desert. They were an earthbound people, tied to the harsh old land of their birth by a complex of ritual and lore. And both ritual and lore, now, were calling the boy to the hills of the north. For it was the season of walkabout: the season-before-the-wet when, from all over the outback, tribes and individuals were making their way to the sites of the corroborees in the lands that had given them birth.

He got slowly to his feet. "I don't want to go to Tableland."

"Oh, Joey!"

"We won't belong there."

The girl's voice wasn't bitter, merely matter-of-fact. "Where *do* we belong?"

His eyes were on the distant hills. He remembered the stories he had heard at the mission from those who had gone walkabout to take part in tribal ceremonies in tribal land; he remembered too (albeit as through a glass darkly) taking part himself in such ceremonies by the waterholes of his mother's tribe; and the strings which bound him to the far-off land of his dreaming were as evocative as those of an Aeolian harp. "Let's go walkabout, Sarah. Back to the Kimberleys, where we were born."

She had known it was coming, ever since he had asked her about the smoke rings. Yesterday it had seemed altogether out of the question; but now, shaken by what she had dreamed, she began to wonder. Two roads had suddenly opened up ahead; which to take? Her eyes followed her brother's. "But the Kimberleys are close to the sea; must be six or seven hundred miles away."

His mouth was obstinate. "I don't care. I want to go."

"We'd die of thirst."

"Stupid! Nobody dies of thirst in the wet!"

Silence, and the girl plaiting and unplaiting her hair. She was intelligent and blessed with plenty of common sense ("An unusually gifted, thoughtful and attractive girl," the Mother Superior's report had read); but her life in the mission had done nothing to qualify her to make the sort of decision that faced her now. She cast round for a compromise. "Suppose," she said slowly, "we stay here today. If a car hasn't come by evening, it'll mean the people at Tableland can't be bothered to look for us. And if *that's* the case, we might as well go walkabout."

Civilized children would never have thought of it. Primitive children would never have dared it. But Sarah and Joey were "twixt-'n'-betweens," inheritors from both ways of life of that little learning that is a dangerous thing.

There was no car. And in the evening they began to get ready, setting aside a couple of water carriers, a cache of provisions and the tiny collapsible tent which was

standard safety equipment for those who drove in the outback. Then they turned their attention to the stockman. The girl wrinkled her nose. "He ought to be buried."

"Yes, but how?"

It was easier said than done, for the body was too heavy to carry out of the gully and the ground at the site of the accident was hard—stratum on faulted stratum of laterite, sandstone and granite. "I know." The boy's eyes were bright with a sudden excitement. "Let's make him a platform!"

"Oh, Joey! A platform isn't Christian!"

"It's that or nothing."

She had to admit reluctantly that he was right—nothing short of a pneumatic drill would have excavated a grave in the gully. So with much panting and straining they heaved Al Lowson's body onto the top of a pair of upended crates, raising him well clear of the ground so that the evil ones who walked by night couldn't molest his body. Then, with the idea of reading part of the burial service, the girl climbed into the back of the truck to look for her prayer book.

Joey stared at the stockman. He remembered his kindness: the sticks of barley sugar and, at their midday halts, the surreptitious sips of Cooper beer. What he did next he did partly by instinct, partly in recollection of the secret games which he and his friends had acted out in the grounds of the mission. He took his handkerchief and tied it carefully to the top of the burial platform. Then he picked up a sharp-edged fragment of rock. Without

flinching he gashed the lower part of his arm from elbow to wrist; he gashed it again and again, deeply, till the blood ran warm through his fingers and the tears welled up in his eyes. Then he began to wail: the harsh discordant lament which, according to tribal lore, would exorcise the spirits which had caused Al Lowson's death.

The girl came tumbling out of the truck. And as she stared at her brother she felt quite suddenly as though she were being torn physically in two; as though half of her was standing dry-eyed beside a coffin intoning the requiem Mass, while the other half was dancing naked and streaming blood round a gaily decorated platform to the thud of didjeridoo and drum. For a terrifying moment she didn't know which body she belonged to; then, desperate to disown the Aboriginal part of her as something to be ashamed of, she began to fumble through the pages of the prayer book. "I am the resurrection and the life," she read. . . . "He that believeth in Me, though he were dead, yet shall he live: and whosoever liveth and believeth in Me shall never die."

The sun blazed out of a copper sky; the handkerchief streamed white in the breeze; and the boy's keening ebbed and flowed in a discordant lament between the mellifluous cadences of Saint John.

Half an hour later, in the pale gold light of evening, they set out to walk to the Kimberleys: the longed-for hills of their dreaming, whose pastures green lay somewhere far beyond the horizon. It was merciful they didn't realize that they had about as much chance of getting there as an ant of crossing the Sahara.

Chapter 3

The evening light was limpid as Sauterne as the children headed into the desert.

The boy led. He didn't look back, for all his attention was concentrated on picking the easiest route through sand-ridge, spinifex and salt-pan. But the girl, following, glanced more than once over her shoulder. To start with she could see both truck and burial platform, delineated sharply in the glare of the sun; but after about half an hour they disappeared behind an outcrop of granite. And with their disappearance came a sense of loneliness so

acute that she had to make a conscious effort to stop herself running back.

In the hour before sunset they covered a couple of miles.

They found a good place in which to camp, amid a cluster of eucalyptus trees which rose like pallid ghosts round the perimeter of a depression. They pitched their tent, started a fire, ate an apple apiece and watched the great gold disc of the moon climb up through the branches of the eucalyptus. The outback by moonlight was beautiful, and the children like well-fed animals stretched out contentedly in the warmth of the fire. They were thinking of dossing down when they heard in the distance a peculiar sound: a metallic clatter, faint at first but growing steadily louder. They peered through the trees in the direction from which the noise was coming, and saw a pinhead of light inching in little unco-ordinated jerks across the skyline. It was some time before they realized what it was: a car coming up from The Granites. After a while the noise stopped and the light came to rest—they presumed by the wreck of the truck.

The girl's voice was uncertain. "If we ran back—quickly—do you reckon we'd catch them?"

The boy said nothing, but very carefully drew sand and ash over the fire, extinguishing even the faintest glimmer of flame. They stood in the darkness, watching; and after what seemed a very long time the pinhead of light moved on in the direction of Alice Springs.

An hour later the children were asleep. The boy slept soundly, dreaming of meeting his mother's tribe in the

far-off plateau of the Kimberleys. But the girl tossed and turned, prey to a complexity of doubts and fears. Had they been wise, she wondered, to turn their faces from the world they knew; perhaps it wasn't too late even now to go back? And in her sleep she kept reaching for the water carrier, checking that it was there.

The stars faded; the sky in the east flushed pink as the feet of a flamingo, and the outback took on the vivid pigmentations of another day. First to change colour were the two-hundred foot eucalyptus, gaunt relics of the forests of antiquity. As the sun came over the horizon their pallid trunks were metamorphosed from white to gold, and their oil-laden leaves twisted edge-on to avoid the heat. The sunlight moved lower, gilding lantanas and brigalow as they intertwined in age-old rivalry; then it moved lower still, warming the furrowed ironbark and the dried-up banks of the everlastings. Finally it flooded into the tent.

The boy woke all-of-a-piece and within seconds was up and resurrecting the fire. But the girl took her time. For a while she lay on her side, basking in the sun and admiring her brother's activity; then she plaited up her hair and sorted out two peaches, a handful of raisins and half a beaker of water for breakfast.

As they ate, the boy's eyes were on the hills. "How long'll it take us, Sarah? To get there?"

"Three or four days. Maybe more."

"I reckon there's bound to be water there, don't you?"

She looked at him curiously. "Why?"

"I just kind of know."

She was too wise to scoff at intuition. Also she had a concrete reason for sharing his view. As one of the most intelligent children in the mission she was well able to read a map; she had taken a good look at the large-scale reproduction of the Macdonnell Ranges which had hung on the wall of the store in Alice Springs, and she had noticed that north of the stock-route down which they were driving lay a rift valley threaded with billabongs. Just how far away the rift valley was she didn't know, but she was certain it lay somewhere in the direction of the hills. She was certain, too, of the imminence of the wet. It was mid-December; already the rains were overdue; and it couldn't, she told herself, be long before the clear skies of summer gave way to the nimbus-grey of the monsoons. . . .

They set off early, anxious to cover what distance they could before the worst of the heat.

The outback stretched away in front of them, very still and very quiet, like a tired old giant asleep in the sun: a world of vivid colours—jade and emerald, white and reseda, crimson, scarlet and gold—here the dried-up bed of what a thousand years ago had been a lagoon, there a miniature range of grotesquely sculptured greenstone. The birds had vanished with dawn; the snakes and goannas were asleep in crevices in the rock, and already little pools of heat haze were shimmering like quicksilver over the pans of salt.

White children would have been beaten to their knees within minutes. Sarah and Joey kept walking for a cou-

ple of hours. They walked in single file, steadily and
without apparent effort, the boy leading and the girl
treading exactly in his footprints. Instinct helped them,
warning them to give a wide berth to colonies of termites and belts of thorn. But though they managed that
morning to keep out of trouble, they missed several op-
portunities of implementing their water and food. They
came to a nest of repletes; children brought up in the
desert would have unearthed the bizarrely swollen ants
and squeezed the honey out of their bodies, but Sarah
and Joey passed the repletes by. A little later the boy
spotted a puffed-up toad burrowing in a depression; a
child of the desert would have wrung the toad dry of
water, but Joey looked at it doubtfully and decided it
wouldn't be good to eat. They did, however, know
enough to dig for yams. They found them in the shade of
an outcrop of granite where they stopped at midday. It
was the boy who spotted them. With his long pre-
hensile toes he scratched at the telltale protuberances in
the sand. "Hey, Sarah! *Worwora!*" Within seconds they
had unearthed the soft tennis-sized balls, the yams whose
flowers and leaves grew under the ground, drawing from
the soil the sustenance which the air of the desert denied
them. The children dug eagerly, following the skeins of
underground foliage till they came to the edible roots.
They collected half a dozen *worwora*, which the girl
added gratefully to their stock of provisions. Then they
stretched out in the shade.

It was the hottest part of the day, and the desert slept
in the sun. Nothing moved except for a solitary dust

devil which spun through the spinifex, a little ball of sucked-up vegetation bobbing about in its wake. The children dozed.

In mid-afternoon, in the hour when even the goannas were panting, the girl spotted a small black speck in the sky to the west. It came rapidly nearer, and a vibrating hum—like the swarming of bees—brought a shower of leaves cascading out of the humble bushes.

The helicopter was flying at three hundred feet, and it passed within half a mile of them. If they had lit a fire, or even run into the open and waved, they would have been seen. But the boy lay still as a chameleon in the shadow of the rocks; the girl wasn't good at making a snap decision, and the helicopter was flying fast. Its next line of search took it several miles to the south, and soon it was no more than a pinpoint on the horizon, and the desert once again lay silent under the sun.

"Joey!"

He half expected recriminations or tears. But she simply picked up her water carrier. "We'd best," she said, "be moving."

All afternoon the sun blazed down with tropic intensity, flinging out great hammer blows of light; but the children walked on, relatively unconcerned, at a steady well-oiled lope, and towards evening the sky turned green as mint and a welcome breeze came softly out of the north. They covered fifteen miles that day. When, however, they pitched camp in the twilight, the hills didn't look a great deal nearer.

They set up their tent on the edge of a desiccated swamp, ate a supper of baked *worwora* and biscuit, and turned in early. The boy would have been content to sleep in the open, but to the girl their tent was a link with the past, a reminder of a way of life from which she was loth to cut adrift. Once inside, they closed the flap to keep out flies and mosquitoes and curled close to each other for warmth. The biscuits had made the boy thirsty, and after a while he reached for his carrier.

"Steady, Joey," she said, "with the water."

They didn't get to the hills the next day; or the next or the next or the next. It was not until late in the evening of the sixth day that they reached the foot of the four-hundred-foot escarpment which rose like a gargantuan red-walled city out of the plain.

They had hoped to find a billabong at the foot of the escarpment. But of water there was no trace.

They pitched camp about a hundred yards from the foot of the cliffs. They were exhausted, thirsty and all too conscious now of the fact that they had bitten off a great deal more than they could chew. The realization of this had been growing on them slowly for days. Now at the foot of the escarpment it finally hit them. They were so small and insignificant: a pair of ants traversing the sands of time, aliens lost in a vast red waterless world.

"Sarah!" The boy kept moistening his lips. "What's happened to the river?"

"We'll look for it tomorrow."

"But *where?*"

"We'll find a way," she said slowly, "to the top of the cliffs. I reckon we ought to see it from there."

For a while this seemed to satisfy him. But later, as they lay curled up in their tent, he was restless.

"What's the matter, Joey?"

His voice was frightened. "We're not going to die, are we?"

"What a silly idea," she said quickly. "Of course God wouldn't leave us to die."

She said it automatically to comfort him, but she was none too sure that it was true. God, presumably, didn't want anybody to die; and yet die people did, especially those who were silly enough to go wandering into a waterless desert. She lay awake for a long time, watching the patterns of moonlight and trying to work things out. Ever since they had been left (when she was seven and Joey four) at the mission, she had been both mother and sister to him: she mustn't, she told herself, fail him now, now that he needed her love and protection as never before. She bent over him, making sure that he was asleep. Then she picked up their water carriers and crawled quietly out of the tent. In the pale cold light of the stars she unscrewed the plastic caps. Her container was nearly a third full, but Joey's was virtually empty. Very carefully she poured half the water from her container into her brother's.

They neither of them slept as well as usual that night, and dawn was welcome.

After they had eaten the last of their apples and a

handful of nuts, the boy unscrewed the cap of his water carrier. His eyes widened. "Hey, Sarah!"

"What's up?"

"I didn't have this much water. Last night."

"You must have."

"No, honest." The boy was insistent. "There was only a drop at the bottom. And now look."

She peered into the container. "Lucky you!"

"Oh, Sarah! You haven't given me yours?"

She took his hand. "Did you remember your prayers last night?"

"What's that to do with it?"

"You prayed for water, didn't you? It must be a miracle."

His eyes opened wider still. "I don't believe it!"

"Come on," she said. "If we sit here arguing we'll *never* get to the top of the cliffs."

They set off along the foot of the escarpment.

It rose almost sheer from the plain: a wall of smoothly fluted redstone, devoid of vegetation and bleaker by far than the desert through which they had walked. The boy shivered. "We won't find water *there!*"

"You never know. Let's look for a way to the top."

After a couple of hours they spotted the dark line of a gully running in a diagonal slash from base to summit. It turned out to be the bed of a river. In the wet the gully would have been a seething turmoil of mud-red water; now it was dry as dust. They climbed about a third of the way up, then rested in the shade of an overhang, looking down at the outback.

It lay silent in the heat of the sun: a sleeping wilderness, waiting patiently for the annual rain which would spin its cycle of life on one more creaking round.

But of rain there was no sign.

Even the wisps of cirrus had disappeared.

It took them four hours to climb the rest of the gully; four hours of clawing past boulders, dried up waterfalls and pools knee-deep in dust. Then suddenly the rocks ahead splayed out to a blueness of sky.

It was evening as they climbed panting onto the rim of the plateau and stood staring in silence at the country which lay to the north. It stretched away in front of them, bathed in the soft gold light of a dying sun: a magnificent panorama, mile after hundred square mile of salt-bush, spinifex and strangely desiccated rock. And in the distance, pools: pools of glinting, shimmering light which wavered and contracted, now flooding almost into the foreground, now retracting to hang a fraction above the horizon. For a moment the boy was exultant. "Look, Sarah! Lakes!" But his words petered into a frightened silence, and he reached for his sister's hand.

She pulled him close to her, pressing his face to her breasts. "Don't look," she whispered. For she knew what the pools of silver were: the salt-pans of the great Australian desert; the mirages which dying men in the grip of delirium go scrambling after but never reach. She ran a hand through his hair. "Don't worry," she whispered. "We'll find water somewhere. I know."

They climbed a little pinnacle of rock and scanned

the plateau methodically section by section, but of valley or depression there was no sign, and after a while their attention was taken by the clouds. They floated low over the surface of the plateau like ghostly warships in line astern: about a dozen puffs of cumulus in gunmetal-grey strung out in an almost dead-straight line. At first the children thought they were motionless, but when they looked more carefully they saw that the clouds were in fact continually rising and falling, their lower layers being pushed upward and their upper layers dispersing in the cool evening air.

"What funny clouds!"

The girl was frowning. Locked away at the back of her brain there was, she felt sure, an explanation of the clouds' peculiar formation. But she couldn't think of it now. And clouds like that, she told herself, were hardly big enough to carry rain. "We'd better," she said, "look for a place to camp."

They didn't talk much as they pitched their tent; for anything they said seemed either trivial or trite. For supper they ate the last of their *worwora* baked in ash; then they dossed down in silence. They both knew that if they didn't find water within forty-eight hours, they would die.

For the second night running they slept badly, especially the girl. Hour after hour she tossed and turned in a fever of anxiety, until at last she crawled out of the tent and knelt by the quietly smoking fire. Please, God, she prayed, lead us to where there's water. As much water as we want. Tomorrow.

Chapter 4

The pardalote came flying low up the gully. It saw the tent and the smoke from the fire, and alighted in a flurry of wings on a buttress of redstone. It cocked its head, its eyes filled with tears, and a heartrending cry echoed and re-echoed among the rocks. "It-isn't-yours," the pardalote wailed. "It-isn't-yours!"

The children woke.

The boy sat up, rubbing his eyes. He ran a tongue round lips that were sandpaper dry and reached for his water bottle; then, remembering, he sat very still. The girl watched him. She had been dreaming; what about she

wasn't sure, but she had an idea it was something to do with the clouds.

For breakfast they ate a couple of *mungaroo* grubbed up from the bed of the gully, and drank exactly half of their water. The boy was surprised that his sister poured so much into his beaker. "You reckon we ought to?"

"It's all right," she said firmly. "We're going to find the river today. I know."

By eight o'clock they had broken camp and were standing on the rim of the plateau looking north over the vast mosaic of ochre, scarlet and gold. The little puffs of cumulus were no longer in evidence, but in their place lay a miasma of mist-cum-cloud snaking lianalike across the plain. The girl stared at it, puzzled, shading her eyes against the glare of the sun.

"Which way do we go?" The boy's voice was anxious.

The pardalote, all this time, had been watching them. Now he came swooping low over their heads. "It-isn't-yours. It-isn't-yours!" His mournful wail faded *diminuendo* to silence.

"Sarah!"

"What?"

"Pardalotes live near water!"

He was, she remembered, right. Pardalotes were birds with an abnormal thirst; they drank eighty to a hundred times a day, and not by the normal process of imbibing through their beaks, but by settling on top of the water, spreading their wings and absorbing liquid through the delicate membrane of their skin. And it was because the pardalotes needed water so badly that they often tried to

warn intruders away, not realizing that by their very anxiety they sometimes led others to the billabongs they were trying to hide.

"After him, quick!"

They darted into the waist-high spinifex. And the pardalote flew at them, beating his wings, wailing like a furious child.

They followed him through salt-bush, thorn-scrub and dust-bowl, past fading banks of parakeelia and the gaunt, eroded headstones of a cemetery of termites. They followed him deep into the plateau, while the sun climbed high into a brazen sky and heat pulsated back from the rocks like the blast from a furnace. They dared not stop. A couple of times they lost him, but by casting round first in one direction, then another, they picked up his trail: a trail not of footprints but of angry laments. He was leading them, they realized, straight for the belt of mist-cum-cloud which hung close to the surface of the plateau about a dozen miles ahead.

They were so busy following the pardalote that it was some time before they noticed that the mist-cum-cloud was beginning to rise and coagulate into the same strange formation that they had noticed the evening before. "Look, Sarah"—the boy came to a halt, panting— "there's those funny clouds again." A pause, then proudly: "I know what they are. Cumulus."

She stood very still. For she remembered now what she had dreamed: that she was back in the hall of the Melville Island mission listening to the voice of their geography teacher—"And in hot climates, cumulus

clouds often form over rivers and lakes. What happens is very simple. The moist air of the river or lake is drawn up by the warmth of the sun, and when it gets to a certain height it condenses in the cooler air and forms into pretty white clouds that are known as cumulus." She unscrewed the cap of her water bottle and poured a couple of inches into a beaker. "Joey?"

"Sure it's O.K. to?"

She smiled. "Sure as I'm sure we're standing next to each other. I told you God wouldn't leave us to die."

It took them the rest of the day to reach the rift valley, and by the time they were climbing the ridge that over-looked it they were covered with dust and soaked in sweat, their muscles were knotting with cramp and their water carriers were empty. But the ridge was green with lichen and swept by a cool and moisture-laden wind. "Steady at the top." The girl's voice was hoarse as a kookaburra's. "There may be a cliff."

A final heave onto a ledge of laterite, and they stood hand in hand staring into the valley below.

It was a deep, steep-sided rift valley, splitting the plateau like the cut of an axe. Its details were veiled in cloud; but there was no mistaking the reseda green of the trees or the silver glint of the billabongs.

A leap of joy, a shout of delight, and the boy was glis-sading fast down the scree. For a moment the girl's fingers ran over the gold of her crucifix. "Thank You," she whispered. "Oh, thank You, thank You." Then she was tearing after her brother, leaping from rock to rock,

slithering down into the valley in a cascade of debris and dust. She overtook him among the nut-brown drifts of the maidenblush, she grabbed his hand and together they flung themselves into the shallows and drank and drank and drank.

The pardalote alighted a little way up-billabong; he spread his wings and watched, in angry silence, the children drinking his water.

"Joey!" The girl's eyes were sparkling. "Don't drink so much! It-isn't-yours! It-isn't-yours!"

He showered her with spray, laughing, and struck deeper into the billabong. She dived under the surface, grabbed his legs and ducked him; and happy as seal pups they rolled over and over with shrieks of delight, while the sun played hide and seek with the cotton-wool clouds, and swamp-coots, egrets and bitterns took off in a great white avalanche of surprise.

An hour later they were stretched out naked on the rocks at the water's edge. The sun was warm, the trees were green, the light was clear and a family of long-legged jacanas* were walking in single file across the billabong. So this, the girl thought, is paradise.

---

* The jacanas, the legendary Jesus birds, don't really walk on water; with their huge webbed feet they use the underwater lily-leaves as stepping stones.

Chapter 5

It was enough at first that they were alive; that they had shade to rest in, food to eat and water to drink. For a couple of days they hardly moved from the billabong; content to laze in the sun, they grubbed up the occasional *mungaroo* and drank and drank and drank. Not until they had recuperated both physically and mentally did they think of the future.

The boy was in favour of pushing up-valley toward the north, but the girl was adamant. She realized better than her brother just how lucky they had been, and she

had no wish to try conclusions a second time with the outback. "We'd be mad," she said, "to go on."

His mouth drooped. "Then what do we do?"

"Stay here."

"For the rest of our lives?"

"Maybe," she said, "someone'll find us. Or maybe we can move on later; after the wet."

He kicked impatiently at a tussock of spinifex. "What's happened to the wet? It ought to be raining *now*."

She looked at the puffs of cumulus. "It'll come. But till it does we stay right here, where there's plenty of water and plenty of food."

He was digesting this without a great deal of enthusiasm when they spotted the naloonga, the black-headed ducks nosing in line astern through the reeds. The girl's tongue ran involuntarily over her lips. "I wouldn't mind one of *them* for dinner!"

The boy was on his mettle. "I'll get one."

"Bet you don't."

She watched intrigued as he collected an armful of reeds and grass which he bound together with lianas and fixed in a makeshift crown on his head. Then he selected a hollow reed, and inserted one end into his mouth and the other up through the tussock of grass. He crept up-billabong, and about a hundred yards from where the naloonga were feeding slid quietly into the water. Ducking under the surface and breathing through the hollow stem of his reed, he began to drift slowly towards the ducks. And—rather to his sister's surprise

—he turned out to be blessed with the hunter's greatest attribute: patience. He took all of twenty minutes to come drifting along like a patch of waterlogged foliage, until he could see, only a little above and ahead, the five pairs of webbed feet dangling from the surface like socks from a line. At the last moment the drake, sensing danger, took off with a tuck-tuck-tuck of alarm; but one of his progeny, slower-witted than the rest, was seized by an upthrust arm, dragged underwater and wrung by the neck until it was very definitely dead. The boy waded ashore and tossed the still-twitching body to his sister.

"Well done, Joey!" Her eyes were shining. "We shan't starve while *you're* around!"

It took them the rest of the evening to pluck and bake the naloonga. It was the first meat they had tasted for more than a week, and they sat up late, picking the bones as dry as last season's yacca, while smoke rose pencil-straight through the gums and the moon lifted clear of the hills. It was a night to savour; warm and soft and full of little movements and sounds—the occasional splash as a fish jack-knifed out of the water, bitterns mooing among the reeds, and from the depth of the rain forest the cry of the brain-fever-bird, a fluted, longdrawn coo-ee, haunting as an invocation to the moon. The girl's toes traced a skein of gold in the billabong. "Let's swim."

The garden of Eden, she thought, as they played tag in the moonlit water, had its serpent; but I don't believe there's a serpent here.

The prospect at first seemed near-idyllic. The valley was theirs and all that was in it: the fruits of the rain forest, the *barramundi* of the stream and the fowl of the lagoons—the piedgeese, dabchicks and egrets which nested in their tens of thousands among the tamarisk and everlastings. But it wasn't long before the children became aware that a shadow was hanging over their Eden.

Indications of this shadow had been there for those who had eyes to see, from the moment they first set foot in the valley, but it was only bit by frightening bit that Sarah and Joey pieced the evidence together. . . .

"Come on"—it was the morning after they had feasted on the naloonga, and the boy was eager for adventure —"let's explore."

They left their tent in the shade of the heartleaves and made their way down-valley.

To start with they followed the billabong as it looped along like a tired old snake between cliffs of redstone; but after a while, egged on by a mixture of curiosity and awe, they gravitated to the forest.

It lay in a narrow belt between cliffs and river, where rainfall was heaviest, its close-packed cassia, sycamore and tulipwood soaring high out of a charnel house of decomposing vegetation. The children had never seen anything like it: so fantastic a battleground of tree and parasite and vine, with the giant dodders and jikkas choking the life out of all that they touched with tourniquet arms, and the bodies of the vanquished rotting at their conquerors' feet like the hulks of so many ships.

The boy's nose wrinkled in disgust. "What a lot of stinking old trees! And half of them dead!"

The girl bent down to examine a tangle of branches, their once-emerald green now faded to a lusterless dun. "I reckon they're short of water."

The significance of what she said didn't strike fully home at the time, but there did pass through her mind a whisper of unease, an embryo awareness of the shadow (no bigger as yet than the spread of a hand) in the otherwise cloudless sky.

It was thirty-six hours before they stumbled on the next piece of evidence. . . .

It was noon of the following day and they were pushing up-river through bank after bank of dried-up everlastings when they heard the waterfall; not the thunderous roar of a Niagara, but a mellifluous fluting like the reeds of Pan. Their pace quickened, and as they rounded a bend the girl caught her breath. "Oh Joey! It's beautiful!"

Even the matter-of-fact little boy was impressed. "Good spot for fishing."

About a hundred yards from where they were standing the river cascaded over a ledge of granite. It was quite a small ledge, not more than ten feet high, and the water came over it quietly, here in little trickles of white, there where the granite had been worn away, in smoother fluxes of green. At the foot of the ledge was a pool of emerald, very still and very deep, out of which the billabong went looping away down-valley in a series of lagoons. The lagoons were white with birds, and their banks a

mosaic of tamarisk and everlastings, while from a grassy mound at the foot of the fall rose a lone cassia, its quinine-producing roots dug deep into the fertile soil.

"Splendid place for a camp."

The boy nodded, his eyes on the waterfowl and the little widening ripples where fish were jumping in the lagoons. "Let's go back for the tent."

It was late that evening, while they were busy constructing a hearth out of blocks of granite, that they heard the noise: no more than a whisper at first, but growing within seconds to the rumble of a miniature avalanche. They stared down-valley, and saw little streamers of sand being blown away in the wind. A section of the river bank had collapsed.

In the rose-gold light of a dying sun they climbed down to inspect the damage. About fifty feet of sand dune had toppled into the river. Not a very terrible occurrence, it seemed, until they began to ask themselves why. The boy stared at the drifts of uprooted everlastings as they floated away in the stream. "They're all dead!"

The girl nodded. And suddenly, in a moment of hindsight, the sequence of events became clear. The level of the billabong had dropped; the everlastings, deprived of water, had died; and the sand dune, deprived in turn of its network of roots, had collapsed.

So here, as in the rain forest, the springs of life were running dry. "We'd better," she said, "go back and finish the hearth. Before it's dark."

She kept her fears to herself, and next morning they started to build the fish trap: the trap which, when completed, was to provide the final link in the chain of evidence.

The boy was up with the sun, prodding about among the reeds of the uppermost lagoon. "I reckon this is the place."

"For a dam?"

He nodded. "Fish can't jump the waterfall, see. So they'll collect here. And if we block the exit they'll never get out."

They gathered together stakes of yacca to mark the line of the dam. The girl was anxious to insert hers in exactly the right position. "Here, Joey?" He nodded, and she pushed in the first of her markers at the very edge of the lagoon, exactly at the confluence of water and sand. The spot was fixed in her mind firmly and unmistakably, as in a photograph: the lagoon lapping the stake.

They worked all day on the dam, finished it by the light of a haloed moon, and the following morning ran down eagerly to see what they had caught. And the first thing the girl noticed was her stake.

It stood a clear six inches above the water.

She stood very still: the fear that in the rain forest had been no more than a whisper was now beating about her like the roar of a storm. Not only was the billabong shrinking; it was shrinking fast.

"Hey, Sarah!" The boy's voice was puzzled.

"What?"

"Something's happened to the dam."

"It looks O.K. to me."

"It's shifted. No, *I* see what's happened. The water level's dropped."

"All the better for catching fish!" She tried to shrug the issue aside, but she could see him working things out and after a moment his eyes opened wide as the flowers of a pitcher plant. "Sarah! The billabong's drying up!"

She started to unplait her hair. "So what? There's still water in it."

"Oh, Sarah! What if it dries up altogether?"

"Course it won't. As soon as we get the wet, it'll be full overnight."

His eyes were anxious. "I suppose there *is* a wet here? I mean like we had at the mission?"

She wished she had paid more attention when they had been taught geography. She had a vague recollection that rainfall in Australia was heavy on the north coast and decreased as one went inland; but she felt sure that even the central desert had *some* rain. She remembered a film, an Antipodean counterpart of *The Living Desert*, which had shown the miraculous transformation which follows the wet: the outback one day parched and virtually dead, the next a rioting mass of flora and fauna—yellow and mauve everlastings, cerise parakeelia, and lizards, finches, marsupials and frogs mating side by side in the life-bringing rain. "The wet'll come," she said. "We've just got to be patient."

It was the quiet times which were the worst, the times when they had nothing special to do, and the fear at the back of their minds came welling up like a mushroom cloud. It was the same fear which, like a premonition, haunted them both: of the water seeping away; of the valley which had seemed so idyllic a haven reverting to desert; and of their being driven on and on in their trek to the Kimberleys till they died in an agony of thirst.

But that evening, as they lay in their tent, the boy found a sort of consolation. "I reckon"—he spoke as much to himself as to his sister—"I reckon we'll be O.K. so long as there're plenty of birds."

"What do you mean?"

"Well, birds know about water. If they thought the billabong was drying up they'd migrate."

She could see that the argument had a sort of logic, but she wasn't all that convinced. She slept badly. And in the small cold hours of the morning she built up and knelt by the fire. Please, God, she prayed, You helped us once: help us again. Tomorrow.

Chapter 6

"Look, Sarah! What a funny cloud!"

The sun had been up a couple of hours and the cumulus was massing for its diurnal march along the rim of the valley: about a dozen puffs of translucent white and one, smaller, of nimbus-grey. Could the nimbus, the girl wondered, be a harbinger of rain, a forerunner of the monsoons sweeping in from the Timor Sea? For a moment hope welled up in her. But even as she stared at the cloud its outline began to disperse and its substance to diminish; soon it had vanished as though it had never been, and the valley lay silent under the sun.

They spent a lazy morning by the edge of the lagoon. It was hot and airless, and even the boy was content to lie in the shade and watch the ever-changing pageant of the birds: the geese and ducks, plovers and egrets which followed one another in restless procession across the lakes. "How long," he asked suddenly, "do you think the water will last?"

"How should *I* know!" The girl's voice was sharper than she meant; for she had been asking herself the same question and had arrived at an answer she didn't like: that if the water level continued to drop six inches a day, the billabong would be dry in a week.

It was a little after midday that they noticed the brolgas.

They had been vaguely aware for some time that about a dozen of the slim grey birds were feeding at the edge of the lagoon. There wasn't at first anything in the least unusual about the brolgas' behaviour. But now, as if at a sudden command, they moved into a circle; one, the leader, took up his position in the center; he unfurled his wings—gracefully as a dancer her fan—and began a stately slow-motion quadrille; and the others followed his lead. In stylized step the birds moved solemnly around in a circle, their feet moving in perfect time and their wings rising and falling to the beat of music which only they could hear. The dance went on for several minutes—more than five, less than ten—then as if at another command it ended, and for a moment the brolgas assumed their original one-legged stance, staring out

over the sunlit waters of the lagoon. Then they took off.

They took off simultaneously in a mighty whirlwind of wings which startled the plovers and egrets to flight. For perhaps half a minute the valley was filled with a crescendo of sound and the sky disappeared in a breathtaking kaleidoscope of black and white. Then the lesser birds alighted back among the reeds. But the brolgas from all over the valley were gone: gone in three stepped-up formations of over a hundred birds which circled once over the lagoons, then headed in a great grey arrowhead toward the north.

The children stood staring after them long past the time they disappeared. The boy didn't say anything, but he reached for his sister's hand.

"Don't worry, Joey," she said. "They may come back." But there was a fear in her eyes that she couldn't hide. For there was no mistaking now what was happening. The billabong was drying up, the trees were dying, the birds were migrating, and their lives—and the lives of every creature and plant in the valley—hung on the coming of the wet.

They were baking a rainbow-hued *barramundi* in the ash of their fire when the boy pointed suddenly up-valley. "There it is again."

The little grey cloud was back, only nearer this time and more clearly defined. It bobbed about on the rim of the hills like a puff of smoke from a giant's pipe, a halo of bluish grey, now dispersing, now mushrooming out

as if reinforced from below. And the girl's eyes opened suddenly wide. "Joey! It's a smoke ring!"

It was the boy who recovered his wits first. He tossed an armful of wood onto the fire, and as soon as the smoke was rising thick and fast through the cassia, he picked up a well-leafed branch and began to swish it backward and forward, cutting the smoke into a series of not-very-expert rings. This, he remembered, was the signal of friendship: the sign that he and his sister were prepared to welcome the strangers approaching their valley.

The girl moistened her lips. "Do you reckon they're white men?"

"Course not. Whoever heard of white fellows making smoke!"

It was a couple of hours before they saw the first of the Aborigines. They had been watching out for them; yet of the tribe's arrival they had not the slightest warning. One moment the valley was empty: the next an *atua-kurka** was staring at them from the farther shore of the lagoon.

---

* A youth who has recently undergone the ceremony of circumcision.

Chapter 7

The boy hopped up and down with excitement. "See him! There, under the heartleaves!" He waved his arms in welcome.

The *atua-kurka* moved into the open. The strangers appeared friendly, but before he beckoned up the rest of the tribe he had to be sure. He forded the billabong, his eyes scanning the crevices of the waterfall and the shade of the cassia. The children watched him, uncertain what to do, until at the last moment the boy, remembering a fragment of both the language and custom of his

tribe, stepped forward. He gestured to billabong and fire. "*Arkaloola?*" he said. "*Yeemara?*"

The Aborigine's face split almost from ear to ear in a grin of pleasure. The strangers, albeit in a language he could hardly recognize, were offering his people water and food. He cupped his hands, gave a melodious long-drawn coo-oo-ee, and before the last note had died, shadows detached themselves from the heartleaves as the myalls came forward in single file.

First across the billabong were the full-grown males, nine of them: thin-armed, thin-legged and wiry, naked and deeply cicatrized, their bodies a burnt-coffee-brown. They took no notice of Sarah and Joey, but drank sparingly from the lagoon (scooping up the deeper water which hadn't been warmed by the sun), then squatted on their haunches to check in the rest of the tribe. Next to arrive were the lubras, girls of nine to fourteen. There were half a dozen of them, broad-mouthed, graceful, lissom and, as is the way with Aboriginal women, darker in colour than the men. They were chattering like bee-eaters about a hive and taking no notice of the group which followed them: the uninitiated boys. Although the handful of boys who crossed the billabong on the lubras' heels were not much older than Joey they would soon be facing the rites of *alkira-kiwuma* and *lartna* (being-tossed-in-the-air and circumcision), and their demeanour was serious beyond their years. Most of the time they trod dutifully in the footprints of their elders, but every now and then exuberance got the better of discretion and they capered about in an effort to attract

47

the attention of the lubras. The penultimate group was the largest, the gins and toddlers: the proven-breeders dangling babies from hip or dillybag, while to the sterile fell the role of chivvying up and carrying the children who were too small or too exhausted to walk.

And last came the medicine man, alone.

He was a commanding figure: an Aborigine of magnificent physique in the prime of life. His authority had no need of trapping or gimmick; he wore it by right of intelligence and birth—for hadn't he the gift of prophecy, and hadn't he for a day and a night been bound to the rainbow serpent by his umbilical cord! As he came abreast of the waterfall he looked at the children, and particularly the girl.

Their eyes met for no more than a second. But it was enough: enough for them both to sense that in a way they didn't as yet understand their lives were bound inextricably together. "*Arvella.*" The medicine man held up his hand. "*Myam purla kapirlipa ngula, miyi ngarlint —jarla.* (Here by the waterfall we will eat and sleep.)"

The tribe made camp, the women preparing fires while the men went foraging for food. They were an offshoot of the Bindibu, a race who, from time immemorial, had led lives of unbelievable simplicity. They had no homes, no clothes, no crops and no material possessions; they simply walked their tribal territory from one waterhole to the next, exhausting one source of food and then moving on to another. The few things that they had they shared: food and wives, children and laughter, tears and hunger and thirst. Their lives were uncomplicated

because they were devoted entirely to the one purpose: survival. It was, among the salt-pans of the central desert, a full-time occupation.

The children watched, uncertain what was expected of them. One difficulty was language. They both had a smattering of their mother tongue, but they found it impossible to understand what the myalls were saying—there being more than three hundred widely differing languages among the tribes of the outback. So they stood hand in hand, not so much frightened as bewildered.

Then Joey spotted the dingo: the half tame bitch, with her progeny at her teats. He ran to her eagerly. "Look, Sarah! Puppies!"

The dingo eyed him without enthusiasm; her hackles rose and her lips curled back in an incipient snarl. But the boy's confidence was disarming; he snuggled up to her, fondling her ears and burying his face in the gold of her fur. "You're sweet," he whispered. "And your babies."

One of the gins sucked her lips in surprise. "*Awhee!*" she called to her companions. "*Binya, binya!*" With a smile she picked up one of the puppies and put it into the boy's arms. He was delighted, tickling its tummy and fondling its ears; and after a while a small pink tongue came hesitantly out and licked the tip of his nose.

One of the uninitiated boys, smiling, nudged Joey's arm and pointed to the lagoon. Language was no barrier. Joey grinned; he put the puppy back at its mother's side, and within seconds the two boys were showering and

splashing each other in the shallows with squeals of delight.

But the girl wasn't ready yet to throw herself unreservedly into the life of the tribe. Keeping half an eye on her brother she made her way down-billabong to where a trio of lubras were diving for mussels among the reeds. She would have liked to join them, but she had both inherited and been taught at the mission a strict sense of propriety; so she simply stood at the water's edge and watched. The girls were not much older than she was but were a shade heavier in build, and one of them, she noticed, was pregnant. In between dives they stared at her, whispering. Their gaze was curious rather than unfriendly, but it was nonetheless disconcerting and Sarah was about to rejoin her brother when the girl who was pregnant climbed hesitantly out of the water.

She smiled at Sarah, walked up to her half shy, half curious, and touched her hair. "*Awhee!*" Her eyes were admiring. "*Budgiroo narran!*"

Sarah relaxed; it wasn't the first time that her hair had attracted attention. She unpinned the plaits and let them fall to her waist; then she unravelled them and with a toss of her head shook loose the auburn-tinted mass of her hair.

"*Awhee! Awhee!*" The lubra clapped her hands with delight. "Kyeema," she called, "Ilarra," and the others came scrambling out of the water. They were enchanted —pure Aboriginal hair being invariably short—and it wasn't long before Sarah was the center of an admiring circle of lubras and gins.

She was starting to show them how to plait the hair into coils when one of the older women who had been preparing food called them to the evening meal. In the general surge in the direction of the hearth Sarah hung back until she spotted her brother, trotting along at the side of his newfound friend. "Hey, Joey!"

He came to her reluctantly.

"Who invited *you* to supper?"

"Gee, there's enough for us all."

"But it's *their* food: they found it, they cooked it. Look, they've even built a new fireplace."

It was true; the children's hearth had been enlarged out of all recognition, and a great mound of mussels and lily-roots lay roasting among the glowing wood and stones of a primitive oven. The aroma—the tang of wood-smoke and of prized-open mussels spitting juice into the flames—made their mouths water. The boy reached for his sister's hand. "Oh, Sarah! Please!"

She hesitated; she was as hungry as he was. "I know." The inspiration came to her suddenly. "Let's give them one of our fish—as a sort of contribution."

They ran to the dam. The fish, perversely, were difficult to catch; but in the end they managed to corner a fat *barramundi* and flick it squirming onto the bank. Then they carried it to the hearth.

The tribe were seated according to the grades of their hierarchy: in front the leader and the medicine man, next the full-grown males, behind and to the left the uninitiated boys, behind and to the right the lubras, and away at the back the babies and gins. As the children

approached, the leader rose to his feet. He was a small, wizened man, with the kind eyes and patient smile of one who has faced up to most of the hardships that life can offer. He accepted the *barramundi* gravely, wrapped it in a bay leaf and placed it at the side of the fire. Then realizing that the children couldn't understand his dialect, he patted them on the shoulder and pointed to the piled-up lilies and mussels, first closing then opening the palms of his hands. His meaning was clear: there was enough for all; the children were invited, indeed expected, to share the Bindibus' board.

It wasn't until they tasted the succulent mussels and the crisp sweet roots that they realized just how hungry they were, and just how inexpert they had been, the last few weeks, in finding and preparing food. They ate and ate and ate.

The leader watched them, smiling. Towards the end of the meal he held up his hand. "*Arvella, arvella! Malata era winyara.* (Listen, listen! I have something to say.)" There was an expectant hush.

"The young male and lubra," the leader began, "speak a strange language, and they have no totem marks on their bodies. We cannot, therefore, tell what tribe they are from. But the hawk and I are agreed they come from far away and are lost. Although small and far from their tribal ground, they were not afraid to welcome us to their valley. Although hungry, they offered us fish. Therefore so long as they choose to stay with us their persons are sacrosanct." With a gesture of deference he drew the children towards him, signifying that they

were under his guardianship. "Whoever shortens their shadow," he said, "shortens mine."

A murmur of approval rose briefly above the honking of dabchicks and naloonga.

The children moved their tent, that night, a little closer to the edge of the lagoon. The boy would have been happy to sleep with the tribe, stretched out by the warming ash of their fires; but the girl was loth to give up her privacy. Also their tent had become a symbol: a reminder that she and her brother were different from the myalls and set store on things beyond their comprehension. For a while they lay awake, watching the tribal ritual of dossing down: the babies being sprinkled with mother's milk and ash and placed in their coolamon cots; the little boys being laid out with their legs straight but apart, and the little girls with their legs straight but clamped together (lest the evil Wulgaru tamper with them during the night); the setting-up of the fragile windbreaks, and the careful segregation of lubras and uninitiated boys.

"Sarah!"

"Hmmm?"

The boy was too excited to sleep. "Can you understand *anything* they say?"

"Only the odd word."

"I tried to ask if they were headin' for the Kimberleys too. But they didn't understand."

"Forget the Kimberleys, Joey. At least till after the wet."

Silence, and a crescent moon swinging gold over a backdrop of cliffs. "Sarah!"

"Hmmm?"

"Do you reckon they know the billabong's drying up?"

"Look!" she said. "I think they're talking about it now."

They were walking up and down by the edge of the lagoon: the leader and the medicine man, their shadows wavering like giants' on the moonlit water. After a while they came to a halt, and the medicine man went down on hands and knees to examine the bank—he was, they guessed, estimating the water's fall. The children watched him as he probed at the dried-up roots and sun-bleached stones, reading from evidence a white man would hardly notice a story as plain to him as if it were printed in clear-set type. Suddenly he sprang to his feet. Dramatically he flung out an arm; pointing: straight at their tent.

In an instant the tranquillity of the night became charged with an inexplicable menace. The boy reached for his sister's hand. "Why's he pointing at us?"

"Goodness knows." She rearranged their mattress of sweet-scented mint. "But I reckon we needn't worry. And it's high time you were asleep."

They lay down, side by side; and after a while the medicine man and his accusing arm became submerged in the limbo of things that it was more comfortable to forget. The moon climbed up through a trellis of stars, the

dingo crept sniffing through the ash of the fire, and the children slept.

Someone was calling her. Calling, calling, calling: from far away and in a tongue that was familiar and yet not properly understood. Obedient to an instinct old as time, she had in her sleep crawled to the entrance of the tent, before her face brushed the dew-wet canvas and she woke, trembling and cold with sweat.

After a while she pulled aside the flap and stared out into the night.

The moon was dying. The great gold aureole of the Southern Cross was turning slowly onto its side. And the medicine man was standing still as a tuatara at the edge of the lagoon.

How long he had been calling her she didn't know, or how or why. Nor did she know what would have happened if she had walked obedient to the billabong. Would they, she wondered, have made love on the moonlit strand, or would his hands have closed round her throat among the underwater reeds of the lagoon?

Chapter 8

It was the sort of morning when the fears that walk by night can't find a hollow in which to hide. The sky was cloudless, little spirals of mist were coiling up in the warmth of the sun, birds and children were splashing side by side in the lagoon, and the myalls' behaviour held no hint of reserve—yams, nardoo cakes and *barramundi* were brought out and smilingly shared. Maybe, the girl told herself, our imagination got out of hand: fear can spread like fire in the shadow of the moon. And yet, even as she tried to reassure herself, she knew in her heart that the things she had seen and felt in the night

were real; as real as the juice of the *worwora* running sticky and sweet over her chin.

The events of the next few days were idyllic. The medicine man took little notice of the children, and it was only in their rare moments of inactivity that they had time to remember the drought; most of the while they lived for the moment, becoming gradually assimilated into the life of the tribe.

It was a life about which they had much to learn; for the myalls who had befriended them were a very different people from the Aborigines of the Melville Island mission. A fragment of the one race on earth whose way of life has remained unchanged since the Stone Age, their daily routine had an almost unbelievable simplicity. They woke to the call of birds: to the cluck of boobooks and the unmelodious screech of the jungle cocks. In the still white light of the false dawn (round about half past five) they pushed aside the windbreaks, and while the men resurrected the fires the women made their way to the billabong for water. The lubras collected it in emu shells and carried it back to the gins. The gins filled their mouths with the water (to make it warm), then squirted it over the babies' bodies, gently washing them clean of the ash and milk which had kept them warm in the night; then they fed them and rubbed their skin with powdered charcoal to give it greater resistance to the heat of the sun.

In this early morning ritual Sarah was soon taking part.

To start with she had hung back, diffident and un-

certain what was expected of her; but on the second day she helped the drawers of water, and on the third day she was given a baby to wash.

"*Mulgari!*" It was the lubra who had admired her hair who thrust the tiny soft brown body into her arms.

Touched by the gesture of confidence, Sarah couldn't show the baby enough affection; she pressed him tight to her breasts, stroked his hair and kissed the top of his head. The lubra was delighted that the stranger so readily accepted the newborn child; and before long the two girls, working together, were rubbing powdered charcoal into the folds of his skin. It was the start of a friendship to which language proved a no-more-than-transient barrier.

The men, meanwhile, had been preparing their weapons for a hunt.

In days of scarcity the initiated males would have been scouring the dawn for food, but with yams, fish and waterfowl at hand for the taking they left the problem of breakfast to the women, and sat at their ease in the sun making yaccawood spears. The boy watched them, enthralled; and he had none of his sister's inhibitions. "Can *I* make one?" He pointed first to the embryo shafts, then to himself.

The leader laughed. He handed the boy a five-foot stem of yacca, a shellful of gum, a wedge of flint and a length of fiber. He liked the little one's keenness, though he didn't for a moment believe that an uninitiated *ambaquerka* could fashion a worthwhile spear. Joey, however, surprised him. He watched and learned from the

others, worked steadily and without stopping for breakfast, and by midday produced a weapon every bit as strong and finely balanced as the full-grown males'.

"*Awhee! Awhee!*" The leader beckoned to his companions. It was the knot that intrigued him most, the running bowline which the boy had used to secure the fiber to the shaft; the leader was amazed that the more he tugged at it the tighter it became. He looked at Joey thoughtfully, and later in the day selected him to take part in a search for emu.

"Sarah!" The boy was breathless with excitement. "I'm off hunting."

"Hunting? Who with?"

He pointed to the leader, the four males and the handful of boys. "Them. *And* I'm taking my spear!"

"Oh, Joey," she said, "be careful."

She watched them as they climbed the scree like a column of ants. She hoped that Joey would turn and wave; but he was too preoccupied with following exactly in the footprints of the myall ahead, and soon he was out of sight.

As they debouched from valley to plateau every member of the hunting party paused to take stock of his surroundings, visualizing each tree, outcrop and depression; for sometime—maybe in five or ten or fifteen years—the tribe would pass this way again, and their survival then might depend on the exactness with which the terrain had been remembered. When he was satisfied that everyone had taken his bearings, the leader struck

out through a belt of sage and thornbush. And it wasn't long before Joey was taught the value of treading in his predecessor's footprints; for the boy behind him, stepping carelessly out of line, got a two-inch thorn through the sole of his foot.

They had been walking for roughly an hour when the leader ducked under cover. He motioned the nearest of the myalls to join him, and for several minutes the two of them crouched in the shadows fixing a ball of spikegrass to the end of a very long string; the string in turn was then fixed to a spear, and the *nulla nulla* was ready for use.

It was a marsupial rat which the leader had spotted: a two-foot bandicoot scavenging for food in the mosaic of spinifex and scrub. Bandicoots are an elusive quarry, but they have their Achilles' heel.

A myall rose quietly to his feet. He swung up the *nulla nulla*, and with a hissing whirr the ball of spikegrass soared high into the air, spinning on the end of its string. The bandicoot froze. In terror it pressed itself to the ground, convinced that the whirling ball was its greatest enemy, the eagle. Petrified with fright, it made not the slightest attempt to escape as a myall walked up to it and cracked its skull with his club.

"*Kurura!*" The leader tossed the bandicoot into his dillybag and set off across the plain.

It was five miles and a couple of hours before they spotted the emus: a flock of roughly a dozen foraging with fussy alertness against a backdrop of tamarisk.

Emu are awkward customers to stalk, for their long

legs give them a commanding view and a surprising turn of speed, while their pipelike and ever-swivelling necks make them resemble so many animated watchtowers, constantly on the alert. But they, like the bandicoots, have their Achilles' heel. Joey watched wide-eyed as two of the hunting party were tarred and feathered as decoys. Covered from head to foot first with the thick black gum of the mindree and then with a layer of feathers and twigs, the decoys were given a false neck and head (improvised from the *nulla nulla*) and pushed into the open. They made no attempt at concealment, but strutted like a pair of ruttish cockbirds straight for the flock; and it wasn't long before certain of the hens began to sidle in their direction. The boy screwed up his fists in excitement as a pair of emu were inveigled closer and closer to the waiting hunters. A signal from the leader, and the yaccawood spears were slotted into the throwing sticks; another signal, and men and boys leapt to their feet and hurled their spears with such accuracy and force that the hens were knocked clean over and transfixed to the sand.

It was a happy and well-laden party that returned at sunset to the camp under the cassia.

The boy was bubbling over with excitement. "I didn't tread on a thorn, Sarah, or snap a twig. *And* my spear's been blooded. Look!"

In the last of the sunlight the children watched the preparations for cooking the kill: the digging of the two great pits, the tipping in of the red-hot stones, and the plucking and spitting of the carcasses. The boy licked

his lips. "Reckon there'll be a feast tonight. But what about you, Sarah? What've *you* been doing?"

The girl's day had been less exciting than her brother's, but not to her mind less satisfying. She had made friends with Thoomee. . . .

She had been staring at the spot where the hunters had disappeared over the hills when one of the lubras touched her arm. It was the girl who had helped her to charcoal the baby, and her eyes were understanding. "*Kurura!*" She led Sarah to the billabong.

At the water's edge two girls were digging for yams. The lubra pointed to them in turn: "Ilarra (Dew-fall)," she said. "Kyeema (Dawn)." Then she pointed to herself. "Thoomee"—her voice was soft and mellifluous as her name, Peace.

When Sarah had got the lubras to repeat her name— "Thara," they called her, since few Aboriginal words begin with an *s*—the four girls set to work collecting yams. The myalls used a *ginyong*, a twisted stick about fifteen inches long, and a dillybag woven from the wood of the string-bark, and they unearthed and stored away the edible roots with amazing dexterity. Sarah's efforts, by comparison, were clumsy and slow, though under Thoomee's guidance she soon began to learn the most likely places to dig and the best way to flick out the tubers. For a couple of hours the girls formed a working bee of their own, and it wasn't long before they were chattering and skylarking with uninhibited delight.

Kyeema was the youngest. Thirteen, strongly built and with fine white teeth so even that they might have

been fashioned by a precision tool from ivory, she tackled every job with rather more exuberance than skill and was a great talker and player of practical jokes. Sarah could tell by the Eaglehawk cicatrized on her thigh that she was a member of the group.

Ilarra and Thoomee, on the other hand, were cicatrized with goannas. The significance of this wasn't clear to Sarah until halfway through the afternoon, when the sudden cry of a baby made them pause in the collecting of yams.

"Ilarra!" one of the gins called softly.

The girl put down her dillybag and running to the cassia picked the tiniest of the babies out of its cot. Very tenderly she guided its groping mouth to the nipple of her breast; then, looking up at her friends who had gathered to watch, she tipped the baby onto its back, proudly drawing attention to the fact that he was a male.

"*Gunnea* (Mother)." Thoomee pointed to her friend. "*Mulgari* (Baby)." Her fingers touched the child.

Sarah nodded.

"*Gunnea*." Thoomee was pointing to herself now. "*Mulgari*." She patted her abdomen.

It was only then that Sarah realized what a child brought up in the desert would have known at a glance: that Thoomee and Ilarra were no longer virgins, but were members of another group who had been exchanged into the Eaglehawks as bearers of children. It was the totemic goannas engraved on their thighs that proclaimed their status. For every myall child, she remembered her mother telling her, was cicatrized at birth

with the totemic emblem of its group. The group who had befriended herself and Joey were, she could see, the Eaglehawks; for every male and youngish girl was marked with the six long cuts that symbolized the totemic hawk aswoop on its prey; the women and older girls, on the other hand, were marked with a variety of symbols (goannas, kookaburras and marsupial cats; wallabies, honey ants and platypus) for they had been purchased from neighbouring tribes at the time of corroboree. This annual exchange of nubile females was the very cornerstone of Aboriginal life—for mating within a group was taboo on pain of death. Of her newfound friends, Sarah realized, Ilarra already had a baby, Thoomee would have one soon, and before long the thirteen-year-old Kyeema would be bartered for the girl of another tribe.

She stood very still, puzzled. Where, she asked herself, was there room in such a pattern of life for the things white women had taught her to value: the freedom to choose a husband, the love and sanctity of marriage? For a moment she felt again (as she had felt by the wreck of the Landrover) as if she was poised between two worlds: two worlds too far apart to be bridged. She watched Ilarra squirting a circle of milk around her baby's cot as a talisman against the molesting spirits, and wondered if she one day would be doing the same. And the thought appalled her.

She was thankful when Thoomee, who had been watching her curiously, gestured to the billabong. She nodded. She pinned up the plaits of her hair. "Race you."

She pointed to the forest. And the two girls, supple as seals, struck out through the sun-warm water.

The forest, as Sarah had hoped, was a refuge: its mysteries were analgesic, its wonders an anodyne to the doubts which had begun to stir at the back of her mind.

She would have been afraid, by herself, to do more than skirt the forest's edge; but Thoomee struck confidently into its heart, forcing a way through the tangle of creepers, parasites and vines and scrambling over the jikkas and dodders which clawed skyward in search of the life-giving sun. The trees were magnificent: graceful blue-gums soaring to two hundred feet, coral trees festooned in rose-pink bloom, kurrajongs like weeping cascades of ivy, domatias aglow with scarlet fruit, and the occasional baobab, "most extravagantly droll," as wide as it was tall and with water stored cool and sweet in its grotesquely swollen trunk. At first the forest appeared to be deserted apart from the birds; but before long Thoomee was unveiling life from the shadow of almost every twig and stone. She levered up a moss-covered rock, and there were the sugar ants, feathery-legged, scarlet-headed and immersed in their ritual of communistic life. For some quarter of an hour the girls watched them, trying vainly to unravel the pattern of their frenzied activity; then Thoomee put back the stones, carefully, as a child might close the covers of an enthralling book into which she has been privileged to look. A few minutes later they found the beetles clinging upside down to the leaves of a boronia. The beetles glowed like specks of phosphorus, their wings veneered

in silver, emerald and gold, and the girls placed them on one another's arms to make mobile bracelets as beautiful as composites of jewel. Thóomee soon realized that the rain forest was virgin territory to her friend, and she drew attention to its wonders with the relish of a connoisseur. She pointed out the fisherman-spider lowering his thread of sweet-scented saliva, then when the bait was taken, hauling it in with the speed of a striking snake, and the flowers of the pitcher plant snapping shut on and eating alive the honey-seeking insects which crawled into the trap of their stamens, and in the very heart of the forest she discovered the nest of a firecrest. It was shaped like a stocking, narrow at the top and so dark inside that the parent birds, returning with food for their chicks, had phosphorescent beaks to light them into the nest. They didn't talk much, though Thoomee now and then repeated the Aborigine name of a plant or bird; but they found that they smiled and laughed and opened their eyes in wonder at the same things, and by evening they were friends.

Light was draining out of the sky as they swam slowly back to the waterfall. And a few minutes after they had waded ashore, the emu hunters came slithering in triumph over the scree.

The feast was all that the boy had hoped for, and more. The emu cuts were succulent, children played late by firelight at the edge of the lagoon, and an old man sang softly of the Dreamtime to the beat of didjeridoo

and drum. It was midnight before the children dossed down.

"Sarah!" The boy was too keyed up to sleep.

"Hmmm?"

"Hasn't it been a wonderful day!"

She nodded. The days were fine. It was the nights that she wasn't so sure of. For with the coming of darkness the atmosphere seemed to change, to become charged with an aura of suspicion and fear. She couldn't think why. She told herself at first that she was imagining things—transferring to the myalls doubts which were in fact her own—but a thousand and one little incidents proved her wrong: the averted glance, the whispering, the sucking-in of lips. Something was off-key. She could sense it now, through the wall of the tent. On impulse she pulled aside the flap.

The medicine man was watching them.

He stood motionless by the lagoon, at a spot where their tent was silhouetted against the light of the fires and their every move was thrown into clear-cut relief. "Why?" she whispered. "Why?"

"What's the matter?"

"Nothing. Let's go to sleep."

He tried to, but he was too tired to relax. He tossed and turned and rucked up the mattress of mint. "You awake, Sarah?"

"Hmmm!"

"We *are* going to stay with the myalls, aren't we?"

"I suppose so—as long as they want us."

" 'Cause I reckon they'll be moving soon."

"How do you know?"

"I've been talking to one of the boys—Bunaro, his name is. Course, I can't understand *much* of what he says. But I think the medicine man's going to try and make rain tomorrow. Then, if that doesn't work, the tribe'll be heading north for the *boree*."

"Make rain! You mean he'll sing to the rain serpent?"

"I guess so."

"Oh Joey! That's a lot of mumbo jumbo."

"I suppose it is."

"If we want rain," she said firmly, "we'd do much better to pray."

"I have. And it's not rained a single drop."

She longed to cry, Oh Joey, I know how you feel, because I've prayed too and nothing's happened and I'm as frightened as you; but she managed to keep her voice casual. "It worked before—remember the pardalote and the smoke ring. So let's try again. Together."

They knelt side by side. And as their silhouettes reared up on the wall of the tent, the medicine man sucked in his breath. For as he watched the shadows, black, wavering and intertwined in the flickering light of the flames, that which before he had only suspected seemed to be proved.

Chapter 9

The medicine man was a man of high estate, intelligent, respected and clairvoyant; on his guidance hung the well-being of the tribe. He knew, both by observation and by the powers of his calling, of the threatened drought; what he didn't know was *why*; why the gods were so displeased that they were withholding the annual rain. Or at least he hadn't known until last night. . . . He doubted if there was a great deal of point now in sacrificing to the rain serpent—for it wasn't *his* blood that the gods were athirst for—but tradition demanded

that the gesture be made. So he spent the morning constructing a rain-pole.

In the soft grey light of dawn he set out in search of a kapok tree, and when he had found one he took out his axe—one of the old iron-headed sort, exchanged many years ago at a corroboree—and cut from the kapok tree a straight pole about three feet long and three inches thick; he also collected an armful of fluffy white down from the pods; then he returned to the lagoon. He called a pair of myalls (elderly men well versed in tribal lore) and together they set up the pole at the water's edge and started to paint it. They painted it with red ochre, their brushes fragments of bark which had been frayed at the end. When it was finished the medicine man held out his right arm with the palm facing up; and while one of the myalls painted the lower part of his arm with ochre, the other tied a tourniquet of pandanus leaf over his biceps. The medicine man selected a sharp-edged fragment of laterite, and without flinching plunged the point into a vein on the inside of his arm. Blood, dark and venous, fountained up in a thin parabola and was collected in a dish of coolamon bark. He sat there passively till the dish was three-quarters full; then the elders dipped their brushes into the coagulating blood and renewed their painting. They painted two dark rings round the rain-pole, one a handspan from the top and one the same distance from the bottom; then they took pinches of kapok-down and stuck them onto the blood so that the pole was ringed with gay little

tufts of white. Next they drew four lines of blood from top to bottom, joining the rings, and these too they festooned with kapok. And finally they painted the pole at top and bottom a brilliant gold.

What an hour before had been inanimate wood was now a thing of beauty. And sacred.

The myalls scooped a hollow out of the sand and inserted the pole at a slight angle. It stood there vivid against the blue of the lagoon, the wind tugging its tufts of white, one end pointing to the sky and the other to the underground nest where the rain serpent slept.

They would, the medicine man told them, sing to the serpent the next day. At dawn.

The children woke to the drone of a didjeridoo and the *kump kump kump* of a drum. "What's happening, Sarah?"

The girl peered out of the tent. "Looks like they're trying to call the serpent. For rain."

They hurried to the water's edge, to where the tribe were standing in silent tiers along the line of the shore. The medicine man was prostrate in front of the sacred pole; his eyes were closed, his limbs were rigid, and he was chanting a harsh, tuneless invocation which, according to Aboriginal lore, would go into the pole and down through the earth till it came to the place where the rain serpent was nesting far away. The adults were motionless. The little children sucked their thumbs. Joey reached for his sister's hand. "Do you think it'll work?"

"Shusssh!" It's so much mumbo jumbo, she told herself, sacrilegious nonsense that doesn't mean a thing. But she found her eyes lifting involuntarily to the sky.

She forced herself to concentrate on the beauty of the lagoon and the restless movement of the birds.

In the pale half-light the lagoon was washed with the ethereal beauty of a dream: a stretch of pellucid water, flanked by soft grey belts of paperbarks and distant cliffs rising mauve and unsubstantial out of the mist. And everywhere were birds—so many birds, feeding, swimming, alighting and taking off, that there was hardly an empty stretch of water. They seemed to be more than usually restless. Perhaps, the girl thought, they don't care for didjeridoo and drum. Even as she watched, a pair of pelicans took off in a cascade of spray and sailed majestically away through the rising mist. In the pearl-grey light things in the distance were hard to see, but she *thought* the pelicans disappeared over the rim of the cliffs.

It happened suddenly. One moment the birds were in the water, the next they were in the air.

First to take off were the egrets: a snow-white avalanche skimming the water with a crescendo of wings so loud that it drowned the wail of the didjeridoo. For a moment the lagoon was full of ripples and reflections as the egrets swept low in a frenzied circle. Then sky and water vanished in a breathtaking kaleidoscope of black and white, as ibis, naloonga and jacanas, plovers, bitterns and snipe, dabchicks, coots and jabirus rose suddenly into the air: a hundred thousand birds, soundless except

for the thunderous vibration of their wings. For a moment they wheeled this way and that in a maelstrom of confusion; then in formation after formation they headed through the mist and out of the valley and over the hills, bound for the distant mountains of the north where the rivers never run dry. And mixed up with the dying beat of their wings was the voice of the boy: "Birds know about water. When they think the billabong's drying up they'll migrate."

Drum and didjeridoo were silent. A sound like the sighing of a great wave rose from the tribe. And the medicine man stretched out his arms; for a moment his body arched up as though in a spasm of cramp, then very slowly he rose to his feet. He looked first at the rain-pole, then at the disappearing birds and then at the children. "The serpent," he said, "is angry. Until the breakers of taboo are punished there will be no rain."

The boy reached for his sister's hand. "What's he saying, Sarah?"

"Something about no more rain."

"And why's he looking so crossly at us?"

"If only," she said, "I knew."

The Aborigines of Australia have been described as "unrefined primitives: a race of have-nots."* Yet they are imbued with a natural courtesy and a respect for life from which many so-called civilized races would do well to learn. It was obvious now to the tribe that the

---

* *The Desert* by A. Starker Leopold and The Editors of *Life*.

medicine man believed the children were responsible for the non-arrival of the wet: yet the thought of killing them, punishing them, driving them away or even re-buking them never crossed their minds. For the Aborigine has a horror of violence and the good sense to leave retribution to the gods.

The tribe had few possessions; so when, a little before midday, the leader decided it was time to move off he simply gave the command, and the myalls formed into their order of walkabout and set off along the shore of the lagoon.

Sarah and Joey watched them. The boy moistened his lips. "They're heading north. Towards the Kimberleys."

The girl nodded.

"Come on then, or we'll be left behind."

She didn't move.

"Sarah, come *on!*"

It was Thoomee who made the gesture for which the girl had been waiting. She broke away from the lubras, ran back to where the children were standing and took Sarah's hand. *"Kurura.* (Follow me.)" Her eyes were anxious and she pointed to the lagoon to where Ilarra and Kyeema too were hanging back.

It was as though a great weight had been lifted from the girl's mind. So they do want us, she thought, to come with them.

In single file under a hot white sun the myalls made their way up-valley: the girl with the lubras, the boy with the uninitiated males.

Chapter 10

It was raining in Darwin, great swathes of water converting the Stuart Highway to a two-foot-deep canal. It was raining in Broome, a steady downpour rattling the tin roofs, sluicing down the pearling luggers' decks, and filling the beer bottles in the Japanese cemetery to overflowing.* It was raining in the Kimberleys, a steady

---

* When a Japanese pearl diver dies and is buried in Broome, food and beer (in lieu of wine) are left on the grave for his departed spirit. In recent years the less reverent townsfolk have been known to help themselves to the occasional free drink; so the Japanese now embed their beer bottles in the concrete plinths of the graves.

drizzle turning the parakeelia to a conflagration of cerise and the everlastings to a mosaic of purple and gold. But the rain didn't penetrate the desert. Later, as the monsoon gathered momentum, rain clouds would be forced over the outback; but for the moment they were brought up short, shrivelling to mare's tails in the arid atmosphere before they had opportunity to void.

And the outback suffered.

The stomachs of the sugar ants grew slack, the breathing of the toads grew slower, the puce wet flowers of the mulgawood turned brittle and dry, and the myalls as they trudged patiently up-valley kept eyeing the falling level of the billabong and moistening their lips.

It was a silent world they walked through: silent and dying. They missed the birds more than anything; for of the twenty to thirty species whose cries the day before had echoed over forest and lagoon only the wood-ducks remained, an occasional gaggle darting bewildered through the narrowing lanes of water. And how quickly now the lanes were narrowing. For with its springs run dry the billabong was shrinking hour by hour, sloughing off on either bank great swathes of glistening sand as a snake its skin.

To start with, the tribe followed a trail midway between river and forest, but in the afternoon the valley narrowed and they were forced into the bed of the stream. The going was harder here, and it wasn't long before the very old and the very young began to lag. Immediately the leader slackened his pace, and those in

their prime picked up the toddlers or dropped back to help the infirm.

The day's march ended early at a spot where the billabong disappeared into a swampy morass, and while the children collapsed in the shade, the men went foraging for food, and the women saw to the fires and the making of windbreaks.

Joey was one of the foragers for food. With two full-grown males and a handful of boys he set off into the swamp, the men armed with boomerangs and the boys with a variety of throwing sticks. It wasn't long before they spotted their quarry: wood-duck, a flock of some two dozen feeding peacefully among the reeds. The boys, clutching their sticks, crouched motionless in the marsh-scrub, while the adults, swimming underwater, set off in a silent detour. For nearly twenty minutes nothing happened; then from the far side of the duck came a sound like the whirr of a hawk. The flock moved restlessly. Another whirr (made through the myall's pursed-up lips) and a pair of boomerangs came sailing dark over the water. The duck took off in a frightened mass, bunching together and keeping low to avoid what they thought was a pair of predatory hawks. In a solid phalanx they passed almost directly over the boys, who leapt to their feet and flung stick after stick into the close-packed mass. Five birds, stunned or broken-winged, were brought down and summarily wrung by the neck. Another hunting party came back with three birds, and another with their dillybags heavy with yams. There was food that evening and to spare.

Sarah meanwhile had been keeping an eye on the toddlers who were playing slippery-dip by the banks of a waterhole. It was the ideal place for a mudlark, with a ready-made slide into the water and unlimited ammunition. She was amazed at the myalls' dexterity: at the way even the tiniest children, with a skip or a sway, avoided the mud pies flung at them from point-blank range. After a while Thoomee joined her, and the two girls sat side by side making a net out of vines. For nearly an hour they plaited up the lengths of fiber (like seamen splicing rope), then, when the net was complete, Thoomee began to instruct her friend in the art of making string men—little figures which danced on the end of the fibers like animated puppets. Sarah, with her experience of needlework, proved an adept pupil. And soon with turn of wrist and flick of finger the girls were vying with one another in the creation of string butterflies which fluttered their wings, string hunters hurling spears and string kangaroos adance over imaginary plains. They were almost sorry when it was time for the evening meal.

Sarah half expected the toddlers to protest at the cutting short of their fun, but they followed her back to the camp without demur. And this underlined a fact of which she had been growing increasingly aware: the myalls had a perfect relationship with their children. Not once, she realized, since the Eaglehawks came into the valley, had she heard a child spoken to harshly; not once had she seen a baby in tears. It had sometimes been otherwise, she remembered, at the mission.

The tribe ate at sunset; and as soon as the meal was finished the younger children were laid out in the shelter of the windbreaks to sleep. There was no playing now by firelight, no telling of stories or singing of songs. For a walkabout saps energy.

When Sarah and Joey realized what was happening they too prepared to turn in early.

During the trek up-valley there had been not the slightest hint of friction between myalls and children. But now, as Sarah and Joey put up their tent, they could sense that the tribe were watching them with disapproval. Perhaps, the girl thought, they don't like our tent so close to their fires; and much to her brother's disgust she insisted on moving a little way down-valley. They were pegging out the guy ropes when Thoomee came hesitantly towards them.

"*Kurura!*" The lubra pointed to a banked-down fire beside which Ilarra, Kyeema and the younger girls were curled up like a litter of kittens.

Sarah shook her head.

"I know!" The boy's voice was eager. "They want us to sleep with them. Let's!"

The idea didn't appeal to her. For the tent was their last visible link with a way of life whose values she clung to, a tangible reminder that she and her brother were steeped in customs very different from those of the myalls and by sleeping in it, apart from the tribe, she hoped both to emphasize and perpetuate their independence. This at any rate was what she told herself—though if she had been completely honest, she would

have had to admit that there was another reason for her clinging so obstinately to the tent. It had become a sanctuary: a refuge from the things about the myalls that she feared because she didn't understand. Again she shook her head.

And Thoomee was too polite to try to persuade her to change her mind. She simply shrugged, walked back to the fire and curled up at the side of her friends; within minutes she was asleep.

"Why've we got to stay in the stuffy old tent?" The boy was indignant.

"Because we'd be cold," she said mendaciously, "in the open."

"Bet *I* wouldn't be."

"Look," she said, "we're staying here. In the tent. And that's that."

He knew her too well to argue, so they curled up on their mattress of mint. But sleep didn't come easily. For he was piqued and she disturbed—it was as though she knew in her heart that she was making a quite unnecessary mistake.

They covered thirteen miles the next day: a stroll for the adults, but as much as the very old and the very young could manage in comfort.

In the upper reaches of the valley the billabong was a mere trickle which sometimes had difficulty in bridging the gap between lagoons. There was no shortage yet of water, no thirst and no suffering; but there was an aura of apprehension, an embryo awareness of the propinquity of death.

Though the waterfowl had fled, there was still a variety of food to be had for the taking. Yams and berries were plentiful, fish in the shallowing water were easy to catch, and on the third afternoon after leaving the waterfall they surprised a herd of kangaroos.

They were passing through alternate belts of scrubland and marsh when the *atua-kurka* who was scouting ahead dropped to his knees. On the soft wet soil was a succession of marks like capital Y's, with water still oozing into the hollow impressions. The leader whispered an order, and three of the myalls walked down to a nearby soakage where liquid mud lay deep as the sludge in a boiler. The children watched in amazement as the myalls immersed themselves from head to foot in the chocolate-coloured mire; for several minutes they wallowed about as if in play, scooping great armfuls of sludge over one another's heads; then, emerging like weirdly dripping monsters, they stood motionless in the sun, allowing the heat to bake the mud onto their bodies. Only when they could move without the mud cracking did they set out at a purposeful lope to follow the Y's— the imprints of the kangaroos' hind feet.

They spotted the herd on the farther side of a marshy depression: an old-man leader, two bucks and a handful of females and young; they were browsing quietly among the scrub. The tribe kept well out of sight while the mud-covered myalls worked downwind and gradually nearer. They had closed to within fifty yards before the old-man leader, who was acting as sentinel, began to show signs of alarm. He lifted his head, sniffed suspiciously and stared at the tussock of spinifex behind

which the myalls were crouching. They made no attempt at concealment, but picked up their throwing sticks with their toes, crooked up their arms in front of their faces, and hopped like a trio of nut-brown kangaroos into the open. Their miming had an uncanny plausibility: the shuffling gait, the regular turning of the head and the frequent pauses to browse; and the old-man leader, for the moment, was satisfied.

The myalls never approached the herd directly, but closed in in a series of hesitant zigzags with much nibbling of herbage and scratching of ears. They were less than twenty yards from the nearest females before the leader again showed signs of apprehension. He eyed the queer-looking interlopers first with suspicion, then with alarm, and this time he realized there was something sinister about them. He coughed, stamped out a warning and bounded away. But for a pair of his harem the warning came too late. Before the kangaroos were fully alerted, the myalls with incredible speed had grabbed up and notched their spears and hurled them with such velocity that two of the females were knocked clean over and pinned to the earth. They died with their eyes still open. And their bodies were slung between mulga-wood spears and carried up-river to the site of the evening camp.

The kangaroos were roasted that night in stone-lined pits. And in the feasting which followed there was no sign of friction between children and myalls—until it was time to doss down.

"Sarah!" The boy's voice was pleading. "I reckon they don't like us sleeping in the tent."

"It's none of their business," she said, "where we sleep."

"But I'd *rather* sleep by the fire."

"Listen, Joey"—it was she who was pleading now—"I want us to stay together. In the day we can join in with whatever they're doing. That's O.K. But we *are* different, you know. So at night let's keep to ourselves."

He looked at her curiously. "I reckon," he announced with unexpected relish, "you're scared. Cowardy girl."

"Don't be so silly," she said.

She told him not to be silly, but she had to admit in her heart that he was right. It was the medicine man she was afraid of. Why, she asked herself, was he always prying on them, late into the night long after everyone else had gone to sleep? He was watching them now. She could sense it: his eyes straining to penetrate the canvas of the tent. He was no better, she told herself, than the storekeeper in Alice Springs. In spite of the warmth she shivered.

Late the following afternoon the myalls saw the sign which they had been looking out for: the little circles of smoke coiling up like rings from a giant's pipe at the head of the valley.

It took them another twenty-four hours to reach the site of the corroboree, the rendezvous at the source of the billabong, where from time immemorial tribe had met tribe at the end of their walkabout. And by the time they got there the river was no more than a trickle: so narrow that it could be stepped over by the smallest of the children, and so sluggish that a piece of dropped-in

coolamon bark took several minutes to drift out of sight.

It was a little after midday that they heard the thud of the drum. They lengthened their stride, and by late afternoon were approaching the *boree*, the meeting ground of the tribes. Normally three or four hundred Aborigines would have been camped at the *boree* for the annual ceremonies of initiation and exchange. Now there were less than eighty. The remainder, like the brolgas, egrets and jabirus, had left the valley in search of water.

The Kookaburras and the Honey Ants were the groups who had stayed behind; and they had already started preparations for the initiation of the younger boys. (Under normal circumstances this would have been followed by the far harsher rites of circumcision, incision and ordeal by fire; but the myalls, knowing that in the weeks ahead they would need to be at their physical peak to survive the drought, had decided to postpone these more rigorous ceremonies until the coming of the wet.) The tribes camped side by side; and while the medicine men and leaders conferred and the males went hunting, the women and children intermingled in a babel of gossip.

Toward evening the beat of the drum grew louder.

It had been thudding rhythmically for hours: an insistent *kump kump kump*, subdued at first but now stepped up in tempo and volume. It got on Sarah's nerves. She tried to talk to the Kookaburras and Honey Ants, hoping that their language might be more closely akin to hers; but it wasn't. She looked round for Joey; for a long time he seemed to have disappeared, and when

at last she spotted him he was in earnest conversation with a group of his friends and waved her away. For want of anything better to do she began to put up the tent.

By sunset the *boree* was ringed by a circle of fires and the drumbeat was swelling to a climax.

Sarah moistened her lips. She was afraid of the drum. Its beat was mesmeric, shaking her body with spasms she couldn't account for and her mind with fears and excitements too deep to be brought under control. Miss Sarah Koyama, she told herself, you're a civilized Christian and you've no cause to be afraid of men tapping a piece of hollow wood. Yet she could feel the sweat on her forehead and the excitement astir in her blood.

By the time the moon had lifted clear of the hills the drum was the myalls' master. Obedient to its call they began to form into a circle, their feet stamping, their hands clapping and their bodies swaying to a rhythm old as time. Sarah joined them. She pushed into the circle next to Thoomee, whose gestures, she noticed, were less compulsive than her companions'. They smiled at one another—like teetotallers whose eyes meet as they sip their tomato juice at a cocktail party.

The drumming stopped. Silence. Stillness. A flying fox silhouetted for a moment against the moon. Then a group of boys—those to be initiated—came running into the arena: three or four *ambaquerka* from each of the tribes. And among the Eaglehawks was Joey.

Chapter 11

A veil of red was rising and falling in front of her eyes and she thought she was going to faint. She heard a voice that she didn't recognize as her own: "Joey! No!" Then it swept over her again: the sensation of being divided between two worlds.

It was as though she had two bodies. She could see them clearly: one was swaying in ecstasy to the beat of the drums, while the other, watching, was wringing its hands appalled. For a quite terrifying moment, she didn't know which body she belonged to; then she felt Thoomee's fingers dig sharply into her arm. "*Ngario yarutu*

kapi. Lawatjarri. (It is nothing. It will be over in a moment.)" The lubra's words were meaningless, but their message got through, and the veil lifted slowly from her eyes, and she forced herself to stand very still, watching.

The boys were coming up to the center of the circle. They walked with the humility of the uninitiated, their heads bowed, their eyes downcast and their hands cupped over their genitals. They knelt in front of the drum, and each picked up a stick of pandanus and rested it lightly on the hollowed log so that the spirit of the drum (when played) might pass through the stick and into his body. It was the tribal leaders who took it in turn to play the drum, softly and ritually, while they sang to the boys of the mystique of becoming a man.

Slowly Sarah relaxed.

Her first instinct had been to rush into the *boree* and rescue her brother from whatever barbaric rites he was getting involved in. Then she had second thoughts. The rites appeared to be innocuous (there was none of the sacrificial bloodletting of which she was terrified); Thoomee was obviously trying to reassure her, and her instinct told her that the myalls were a people devoid of purposeless cruelty. So it seemed as if physically Joey might come to no great harm. And mentally? It was very wrong, she knew, to be taking part in a pagan ritual and when it was over she'd have plenty to say to him; but short of making the sort of scene that would get them drummed out of the tribe there wasn't much

she could do about it. So she clung very tightly to Thoo-mee's hand and wondered what happened next.

The drum throbbed into the night, softly repetitive, with each of the boys being sung to in turn, to the clap of hands and the stamp of feet. It was a couple of hours before the tempo changed.

When the last of the eleven boys had been initiated, a new drummer picked up the sticks of pandanus. He beat out a faster and more exciting rhythm, and the boys were led to an outcrop of rock on the farther side of the circle. The rock had already been ringed with a belt of thorn-scrub about six feet high, and as soon as the boys were in position the scrub was set alight to the accompaniment of wails from the didjeridoo.

Sarah found it hard to see what was happening; but as the smoke billowed up, the fears that she had been a prey to came crowding back. The smoke thickened. And as the flames, with a gay little crackle, raced red through the dry-as-timber scrub, she heard a sound which pricked up the hair on the nape of her neck: a half-drowned whimper of pain.

She felt as if she had been doused in ice-cold water. Oh Joey, she thought, what are they doing to you; there on the rock that's ringed by fire and hidden by smoke? She tried to break out of the circle and run to him, but Thoomee wouldn't let go of her hand. *"Binya! Lawatjarrita.* (Look! It is over.)" The lubra was point-ing to the figures now staggering one by one out of the circle of smouldering scrub.

In the chaos of darkness, smoke and pounding feet she couldn't recognize her brother. But she counted the

boys as they burst through the ring of flames—three, four, five, right up to eleven—and thankfulness welled up in her: whatever they'd done to him he had survived.

The circle of myalls broke up, the women forming into a line on one side of the *boree* and the men into a phalanx on the other. One ritual was ended, another was about to begin. But all Sarah cared about was her brother.

As the boys came staggering out of the smoke, they were seized by the youths of their tribe and led away— for now they were no longer *ambaquerka* (a child of either sex) but *ulpmerka* (boys who had taken the first step on the road to manhood and who had for the next few years to live apart from their family and eschew the company of women). So when Sarah eventually spotted her brother he was surrounded by a circle of teen-aged boys. She thought he looked frightened and dazed; he was staggering about as if he were drunk, and holding his face in his hands.

"Joey!" She tried to push through to him. But the boys formed a barrier between them. They waved their arms. "*Koit bau!* (Go away!)" they shouted. Their voices were shocked.

She stood very still. She wanted to mother him; to take him into her arms and ease his pain and share his fear. But she had enough of the myall in her to know that the tribe would consider this not only unnecessary but wrong. She looked for Thoomee to guide her. But Thoomee had gone; gone to the line of lubras and gins asway like reeds in the wind.

She didn't know what to do or where to go. She thought of flinging herself at the boys, kicking and claw-

ing them in the places that hurt most and grabbing Joey and rushing with him into the desert. She thought of leaving her brother to fend for himself and joining Thoomee and the women, and an unfamiliar excitement stirred in her blood. But in the end she simply turned and walked very slowly back to the tent.

It's all I can do, she told herself. Wait. And if he wants me he'll come.

She lay in the dark, her body longing to surrender to the pulse of the drum, her mind anxious to the verge of distraction about her brother—for she felt instinctively that what had happened in the *boree* was the beginning of the end, the first step in his shedding the values by which up to now he had lived.

She didn't dare to believe that he would come to her. She reminded herself of his toughness and self-reliance and the ease with which he had fallen into the myalls' way of life. What she had forgotten was that blood is thicker than water.

After what seemed like a very long time she heard a scuffle; footsteps in the dark; a shadow on the wall of the tent, and he was nestling beside her.

"Joey!"

"It's all right," he said. "Don't fuss."

"What have they done to you?"

"They made a hole in my nose"—his voice was indignant—"like I was a pig!"

She had an overwhelming desire to laugh: it was so much less horrific than some of the things she had imagined. "Lie on your back," she said. "To stop it bleeding."

He stretched out on the mattress of mint. "I didn't cry. Bunaro did. But I didn't."

"Good for you."

"I wouldn't have minded so much, if only they'd told me *why*."

She smoothed the hair out of his eyes, filled suddenly with a happiness beyond the power of words to describe. "Don't chatter. Just lie still."

It was his nasal septum that had been bored through. (Sarah had noticed that all the older boys wore nose-bones, and these, she now realized, were a sort of status symbol, a visible sign that the wearer had started the journey to manhood.) There was still a good deal of bleeding, but the hole looked neatly made and clean. "Stay still," she said. "While I get some water."

She fetched it in an emu shell and started very gently to bathe away the blood. "Am I hurting you, Joey?"

"No."

She wanted to take him into her arms; to let him know that she was proud of him for being brave, and happy beyond relief that when he had needed help it was she to whom he had turned. But she knew that he didn't like too open a display of affection, so she simply squeezed his hand and smiled. And the bond between them was the stronger for not being put into words.

When his nose had stopped bleeding she lay beside him. And he snuggled close to her for comfort, grate-fully, as he had done in the early days of their walkabout when they were frightened and lost. "It's all right," she whispered. "Go to sleep."

He nodded. At first he was restless, tossing, turning

and unable to get comfortable; then quite suddenly he fell into the comalike sleep of those who have been traumatically shocked.

The girl didn't move, but lay listening to the thud-thud-thud of the drum. Its beat was mesmeric, like the pound of monsoon waves on the Melville Island shore. Her eyes drooped, flickered and closed; and her breathing, like her brother's, deepened and slowed. Sleep was an anodyne.

The flap of the tent was ripped violently open.

Silence.

And fear.

And the eyes of the medicine man dark with anger as he stared at the children.

For a full minute he stared at them, condemnatory against the glow of the smouldering scrub. Of the ultimate crime of which he suspected them there was still no evidence. But wasn't what he saw enough?—the lubra and the *ulpmerka* sleeping (even after initiation) not by their separate fires but together, violating the most fundamental tenet of myall lore.* He spoke softly. "*Waru kupalupalu kapi tarnga wapamiyi pirla wariki-diki.* (The white-winged hawk must circle the ironbark forever.)"

She didn't know what he was saying or meaning or thinking. She only knew, as she stared into his disapprov-

---

* In every Aboriginal tribe there are strict marriage laws, laid down with a view to avoiding malformation and insanity. In the larger tribes it is broadly true that "a man marries his mother's mother's brother's daughter's daughter, though this is something

ing eyes, that he was the epitome of all the dark ritualistic things in the myalls' life that she hated and feared. She scrambled to her feet. "Get out." Her voice had the venom of a cornered snake. "Get out, and leave us alone!"

And when he didn't move she sprang at him, her fingers clawing at his eyes.

He ducked, and her nails raked the side of his face, drawing blood.

If she had been a man he would have killed her, but this sort of violence from a girl was beyond his understanding. He backed out of the tent. She is evil, he thought; a breaker of taboos, an abomination to the gods. Until her body lies broken in the desert there'll be no rain.

Joey was on his feet, his eyes wide with fear.

"It's all right," she said. "Nobody's going to hurt you."

For a while they stood hand in hand, trembling. Then the boy, exhausted beyond endurance, collapsed on the mattress of mint. But the girl was too overwrought

---

of an oversimplification" (Colin Simpson: *Adam in Ochre*). In smaller tribes or the moiety of a tribe—such as the Eaglehawks— "a man can never marry a woman of his own group, but must take a wife from another group" (M.F. Ashley-Montagu: *Coming into Being Among the Australian Aborigines*).

It is because of these laws that adolescent boys and girls of the same group are kept strictly apart, eating, walking and sleeping with members of their own sex. Those who violate this code of behaviour are suspected of a crime which has no exact parallel in the Western world, but whose nearest counterpart is incest.

to sleep. Hour after hour she sat without moving at the entrance to the tent, while over the *boree* the drumbeat rose and fell and the lines of the dancers swayed like tamarisk in the wind. At first she was filled with an angry elation—like the bird which has driven a prowling cat from its nest—but after a while her elation gave way to sadness. It's no use, she told herself, our fighting the myalls; somehow we've got to live with them. But how? If only, she thought, we had more in common: if only we could find a link, a bridge which would transcend the differences between us.

Beside her her brother slept. But she lay awake, hour after hour, thinking. And the idea of a bridge came gradually to obsess her: the idea of finding a touchstone which would bring their ways of life miraculously together. She felt certain that such a touchstone existed, though in what sort of shape or form she hadn't the slightest idea. And in the small cold hours of the morning she knelt in prayer. "Please, God," she whispered, "show me the bridge, the bridge that will link us together, the bridge that will make us one."

The drumbeat stopped.

For a moment the women stood very still. Then, as the men in a phalanx swayed closer, they started to chant. "*Koit bau! Koit bau!*" they chanted. But the men held their fingers to their ears so that they couldn't hear, and rushed among them.

Chapter 12

The Kimberleys were veiled in cloud. On the northern slopes nimbocumulus hung heavy and damp, and rain fell steadily hour after hour till the Drysdale and Ord were in spate. But by the time the clouds had reached the southern slopes they were thin and anhydrous; they voided no rain, and the rivers which flowed south into the outback stayed dry as the dust-filled gullies of the moon.

The three groups were close to the limit of Bindibu territory now. The land to the north didn't know them, and it would be wrong, the elders argued, to so much as

set foot in it. The medicine man, however, could remember that years before, at the time of the Great Thirst, a well to the north of the *boree* was said to have held water long after their usual drinking places had run dry. And to this well he decided to lead his people.

The Honey Ants and Kookaburras were more fatalistic. If the serpent wished them to have water, they argued, he would bring it to the *boree;* and even the prospect of death from thirst couldn't persuade them to move from their tribal land. They cut their hair, built their burial platforms and settled down by the dried-up remnants of the billabong to wait.

The Eaglehawks, however, headed north.

In spite of what had happened in the night, no objections were raised as at the start of the walkabout the children took up their places, Sarah among the lubras and gins and Joey among the initiated boys.

The going, right from the start, was hard. No shade —for they soon left the valley and struck out over a featureless plain—no vegetation, no food and no trace of water. They moved slowly, in single file and with none of the skylarking which had enlivened their trek up-valley. It was as if even the children realized now that their survival hung in the balance.

Sarah walked with her friends. She thought at first that Kyeema must have gone on a hunting party or have joined the toddlers and gins who brought up the rear. It was only gradually, as the hours passed and the lubra failed to put in an appearance, that the truth dawned on

her. Kyeema had been exchanged: exchanged for the girl from another tribe who was walking with downcast eyes at her side. Spurred on by the thought of there-but-for-the-grace-of-God-go-I she floundered into conversation with Thoomee. If only I could learn a bit of their language, she thought, there'd be a chance to communicate.

The myall was a willing teacher. To start with she simply pointed to the occasional rock, plant or reptile which they passed and repeated its Aboriginal name; but when she realized that her friend was trying to string together sentences and express ideas she entered wholeheartedly into the job of making herself understood, and before long the two girls were acting out phrases like "Ilarra is feeding her baby" or "the goanna has a long tail," to the accompaniment of giggles and smiles. They would soon have grown tired of it if their sense of humour hadn't been very much *en rapport*.

They covered fifteen miles that day; fifteen miles of dusty grind through a plainful of gibbers—stones which had been rounded and polished by windblown sand to the smoothness of copper discs. By the time the tribe pitched camp they were hot, exhausted and covered in dust. And thirsty. But no one, not even the babies, was allowed more than a mouthful of water from the resin-treated yallahs.

That night in their tent the girl was restless.

"What's the matter, Sarah?"

"Nothing."

"Then what are you muttering for?"

"I'm trying," she said, "to remember words: the ones Thoomee taught me."

"You mean you're learning their language?"

She nodded.

The boy was intrigued. "*I* know some words: *kully koomurra*, that's emu eggs. And *kurango*'s the word for sun."

She nodded. "And *budgiroo* is good and *baal-baal* bad."

"Hmmm! You reckon you'll *ever* be able to understand what they say?"

"Don't see why not."

"Maybe"—with sudden discernment—"you'll soon know enough to ask the medicine man why he's always spying on us."

"I certainly hope," she said, "I will."

The second day was more exhausting than the first. For soon after dawn the tribe was brought up short by a saline swamp: a vast depression which in the wet would have been a maze of waterway and reed but was now dried out to a morass of evil-smelling mud. It took them six hours to cover as many miles: six hours of picking a corkscrew route between belts of decaying reed and pools of salt which trapped and reflected the heat like a prism light. The very old and the very young would never have survived the crossing if they hadn't been helped.

Sarah had noticed before that the myalls were a considerate people and that if one of their group was in trouble the others rallied to help with a selflessness which would have led to the raising of eyebrows in a so-called

civilized society. She had more evidence of this in the depression. For as soon as the toddlers and the elderly began to lag, they were either picked up and carried or helped. And this wasn't a case of parents looking after children or relatives keeping an eye on their folk who were old; for the myalls were untrammelled by ties of family—their unit was the group or tribe, a complex and interdependent organism uniquely equipped for survival. So babies were slung astride hips, toddlers were hoisted pick-a-back onto shoulders, and the old were relieved of their dillybags and yallahs and given a helping arm. And the tribe filtered like a column of ants through reedbed, salt-pan and quicksand, surmounting together obstacles which would have been beyond their compass as individuals. All morning they slithered and slid through the dried-up waterways, bludgeoned by a malignant sun and sinking knee-deep in the drifts of fine dry mud. It was mid-afternoon before they broke through to a kinder terrain: a range of undulating grassland, dotted with spinifex and clusters of sweetly sapped nargoola.

Sarah hoped that they were going to camp among the nargoola, or at least stop for a rest. But the leader walked on. On and endlessly on. And they had to keep up. There was no chattering now with Thoomee; and the laughter of yesterday had been left behind with the smooth, round discs of the gibbers.

Towards evening Sarah noticed that her friend was beginning to flag—for although Thoomee was young and resilient she was six months' pregnant. "I'll take your dillybag," she said.

The lubra wouldn't part with it at first, but when

eventually she was persuaded to sling it on Sarah's shoulder her eyes were grateful.

They camped in the twilight at a spot where a solitary baobab rose grotesquely out of the plain. The myalls tried tapping the baobab for water. But the tree was dry; dry and dying; even its gum had solidified to a desiccated paste.

After the children had eaten and pitched their tent, Thoomee joined them. She laid her hand on Sarah's arm. "*Noolinga.*" She pointed to the east where darkness was falling like fine black dust on the colours of earth and sky. "*Bombura,*" closing her eyes she laid her head on the palm of her head.

"*I* know what she's trying to say." The boy was proud of his perception. "It's dark. An' it's time to sleep."

The girls smiled, bound by an understanding more eloquent than words. Then Thoomee lay down by her fire, and the children in the privacy of their tent.

On the third day after leaving the *boree* the going was easier at first, and in the early morning the girls renewed their language lessons. But by midday thirst and exhaustion had taken their toll; Sarah was carrying her friend's dillybag, the children were glassy-eyed and silent, and the oldest man in the tribe was lagging behind.

He was slight, frail and seventy-eight, and a trachoma had scarred his eyes with granular excrescences so that he could see no more than a couple of yards. He refused to give up. But no matter how many people dropped

behind to help him he could walk only so fast. And no faster. And that wasn't fast enough. Several times the Eaglehawks rested to let him catch up, but eventually and inevitably there came a time when they simply left him behind. For some hours one of the older gins stayed at his side—for she remembered that nearly fifty years ago when she had been exchanged into the Eaglehawks from another tribe the old man had treated her gently; her mind went back to the nights they had lain together under the sweetly scented acacia, and now in the hour of his dying she moistened his lips with her water and gave him the comfort of her arm as she guided his footsteps in the wake of the tribe. The old man knew that he was going to die and was afraid: a little afraid of dying, but more afraid by far of dying alone so that his body would never be hoisted onto its burial platform but would be left for the evil ones who walked by night to molest. Nevertheless he urged the gin to leave him, fearing that she too would lose track of the walkabout and perish. And eventually she touched his eyes with the tips of her fingers, very gently, and hurried after the tribe.

They covered another fifteen miles that day and pitched camp at a spot where great drifts of parakeelia were spattered like blood over the desert. They lit their fires, ate sparingly, and drank their mouthful of water apiece. Sarah and Joey were about to doss down, when the old man came crawling on hands and knees toward the light of the fires.

The myalls ran to him; they carried him into the

shade and laid him at the side of his gin; and she took his head very gently and placed it between her breasts.

Please, God, Sarah prayed that night, don't let the old man die.

But she woke in the false dawn to the sound of keening, and to the clink of stone on stone as his burial platform was raised the requisite three feet above the ground.

She was appalled. What's the use, she thought, of praying to God if He doesn't listen? I might as well pray to Wulgaru.

On the fourth day the tribe were troubled seriously by thirst. Their yallahs were nearly empty now, and the leader had said they were to drink only a couple of mouthfuls of water a day, one at sunrise, one at sunset. It was the newly weaned children who suffered most. And Thoomee.

The girls were speaking by now half in halting Aboriginal and half in mime; and toward midday Sarah held out her water bottle. "*Arkaloola?* (Drink?)"

Thoomee shook her head.

But Sarah was insistent. "For your *mulgari* (baby)." She patted the lubra's abdomen.

Thoomee's eyes softened, and she placed her hand over Sarah's, pressing it to her tummy. "*Ngurtjutjuku,*" she said. "*Pudanyanka kutjaka wahutulu pakani.* (He is all right. Feel how strongly he kicks.)"

They smiled at one another, and Sarah slung the lubra's dillybag over her shoulder, and they walked on and on. Endlessly. Mocked by a pulsating sun and the

mirages of great cool lakes which slid toward them like sheets of mercury out of a heat-hazed sky.

Toward evening the grassland petered out into a succession of sandstone ridges: great belts of arid wasteland, crisscrossed by random faults like the palm of an old man's hand. It was difficult country to walk through, but they had one stroke of luck. About half an hour before pitching camp they unearthed a cluster of *mungaroo*. The *mungaroo* themselves were withered, but their roots were fleshy and had retained a modicum of juice. And the myalls ate and ate and filled their dillybags to overflowing and ate again.

They camped that night in the bed of a wadi, and the leader said they had walked well and that early the next day they would come to the waterhole-which-never-ran-dry. It may have been the *mungaroo* or it may have been the promise of a long, cool drink on the morrow, but they slept more easily that night, and the following morning set off in good heart.

A little before midday the *atua-kurka* who had been scouting ahead was called back, and the myalls went into conference. Only the leader and a couple of the older gins had been to the waterhole before—and that thirty years ago—but with their photographic memory of terrain they were confident they could find it; and sure enough after a couple of hours' casting round the tribe began to head purposefully toward an outcrop of granite rising cairnlike out of the plain. Soon they were forcing their way through a maze of boulders which lay one on top of another in random drifts. The boulders

were veined with greenstone, festooned with arras of maidenhair and interspersed with the occasional ficus, its roots arching out of the ground like the tentacles of an octopus. As they neared the center of the cairn, the ficus increased in size and greenness, and the *atua-kurka* broke into a run.

They came to the waterhole suddenly. One moment they were squeezing through a cleft in the rock, the next they were staring in silence at the saucer-shaped depression.

It was dry as the sand of the Namib.

"*Awheeeessh!*" It was a sound which Sarah and Joey had heard before: by the edge of the lagoon, when the birds in their tens of thousands had taken flight.

The tribe pressed forward in an agony of hope as leader and medicine man clawed out the mud in the lowest part of the depression. They dug and dug. But their hands never got moist.

The medicine man rose slowly to his feet. His voice was accusing, his eyes on the children. "The rain serpent," he said, "is angry. He has taken away our water."

The boy reached for his sister's hand. "What's he saying?"

"Something about the rain serpent."

"Then why's he looking at *us?*"

"I only wish to God," she said, "that I knew." She turned to Thoomee. But the lubra had sunk exhausted to the rocks, her forehead was beaded with sweat, her hands were spread over the child in her womb, and the pain in her eyes made the questions that Sarah was going to ask seem almost trivial.

They found an idyllic spot in which to camp, about a hundred yards from the waterhole. There was shade and wood from the ficus, shelter from a semicircle of granite, and sand to sleep on that was smooth as a carpet of silk. But the beauty of their surroundings was a mockery. For they had barely a mouthful of water left in their yallahs; not enough to slake the thirst they were racked by; nothing like enough to see them back to their tribal land.

Some races would have given way to a frenzy of re-crimination. But the Aborigines have a saying, "If thirsty, why worry? Worry only makes it worse." So the Eaglehawks went uncomplaining about the job at which they were good—surviving—and eventually one of their foraging parties discovered the nest of a scrub turkey. The scrub turkey itself had long since died of thirst, but its eggs formed the basis of a meal.

The moon that night was full and haloed; it flared up among the ficus like a great disc of copper, bathing the camp in a lurid blood-red light. Nobody could sleep. And after a while one of the older myalls began to in-tone a traditional chant of defiance to the spirits of evil and death; the chant was taken up, improvised, em-broidered on and orchestrated with the stamping of feet and the clapping of hands; wood was thrown on the fires; and the myalls with intuitive wisdom settled down to try and forget their troubles in an opiate of story-telling and song. One of the first stories—the legend of the rainbow—was told by the leader.

The Aborigines have no written word, no books nor tablets of stone; their lore and beliefs have therefore to

be passed on from generation to generation by word of mouth in the form of stories. These stories are told by the men, memorized by the women and passed on word-perfect to the children; and for this reason they are told in the simplest of language—even Sarah could get the gist of them, though the nuances as often as not escaped her.

"*Arvalla, arvalla. Yirnan yarra tukurpa yirripura.* (Listen, listen. I have a story to pass on to you.)" The leader stood up, spotlit by moon and fire. "In the beginning," he told them, "was Bunylda, the spirit of the desert. And Bunylda lived in the salt-pans with his six-year-old daughter, Lolari. The salt-pans were dull and dry, and Lolari soon grew tired of the spinifex and the withered grass which were all that she had to play with, and she begged her uncle Tyeera (the spirit of the wind) to take her to a place where there were flowers. So Tyeera picked her up, and carried her across mile after hundred mile of desert till they came to a rain forest. Here he left her, saying, 'Be good. And I will come back for you in the evening.' Lolari walked through the forest admiring the flowers and was happy. She had never seen such wonderful colours: the gossamer clouds of orchids, the wax-white veils of clematis, the crimson of the fire-flame, the golden waterfalls of mimosa and the vivid blue of the jacarandas. She was enthralled. And tempted: tempted to pick the blooms. They will be so pretty to play with, she told herself, back in the desert. So she picked and picked until she could carry no more; then, her flowers in her arms, she sat down by the side

of a stream to wait for her uncle. But Mungolo, the guardian of the rain forest, noticed that some of his flowers were missing. On hands and knees he followed the trail of broken twigs and bent grass, till he came to Lolari sitting, the flowers in her lap, at the side of the stream. 'Wicked girl,' Mungolo shouted, 'to steal the jewels from my forest. I shall lock you for ever in the hollow trunk of a kurrajong!' Lolari was terrified. She screamed. And her uncle, hearing, came swooping down and seized her just in time, and bore her away through the bloodwoods and casuarinas. But Mungolo was not to be thwarted so easily. He plucked a trumpet of convolvulus and blew the alarm; and with an angry roar the spirits of the rain forest sprang into the air in pursuit. In an instant the sky was filled with sound and fury: first the frightened rushing of the wind, then the great dark cloud of the rain people. All evening the chase went on, till in the end the wind outstripped the rain, and Lolari was returned to her home in the salt-pans. But her flowers were gone. For so fast had Tyeera been forced to travel that the fire-flame, mimosa and jacarandas had been torn one by one from the little girl's grasp and strewn in a great multicolored arch across the sky: the rainbow, which to this day springs to life whenever the flowers are watered by rain and warmed by the sun."

The leader sat down. And immediately another myall rose in his place to tell the story of why flying foxes hunt only by night; and when he had finished there rose another, with the story of why women stopped carrying

their babies in pouches like the marsupials. And so the stories went on and on, under a blood-red moon, until at last in the small hours of the morning the medicine man rose to his feet.

"Listen, listen," he began. "For I have something important to tell you."

The myalls stirred, expectant.

The medicine man was a born storyteller; he used no gimmicks or histrionics, but spoke with a natural eloquence. "The ironbark," he began, "grows tall and strong and is sweetly scented. To it come bees, attracted by the scent of its flowers; and the bees swarm and make honey. Now all this is seen by *almakeelia*, the white-winged hawk, who spends her life ever soaring and swooping about the ironbark in an effort to steal the honey. But as often as *almakeelia* swoops low among the branches she is driven away by the sharp-tongued honey-lizard which lives in the bole of the ironbark and defends the hive as fiercely as though it were his nest."

The medicine man paused. "This," he said, "we know to be true. For who is there among us who has not seen the ironbark; and always in its branches the honey and on its bole the lizard and overhead the hawk?"

He paused again. And Thoomee, who knew the legend of the ironbark, reached for Sarah's hand.

"This hawk and this lizard," the medicine man went on, "are spirits. Listen, listen, and I will tell you how they came into being. . . . There was once a tribe. And in that tribe there lived a girl who was wicked. She took to

herself a boy who was one of her own people—blood of her blood and totem of her totem—and the two of them went about together, in defiance of the lore. The medicine man rebuked the girl; but she laughed and continued in wickedness, till the gods became angry. They became so angry that they made the men of the tribe impotent and the women sterile, the hunting grounds they denuded of game and the wells of water. The tribe suffered. One day the medicine man said to the girl, 'Help me to gather honey out of the ironbark.' And they went together to a tree which grew by itself in a lonely place in the desert. The medicine man pointed to a honeycomb high in the uppermost branches. 'You are more nimble,' he said, 'than I. Climb up and knock off the honey, and I will catch it.' So the girl climbed into the iron bark. As soon as the foliage hid her from sight, the medicine man took an axe and began to cut through the trunk. The girl heard the thud of his axe and was frightened; but the medicine man called out that it was only the bark of a dingo. The tree swayed; and again the girl cried in fear, but the medicine man called out that it was only the wind. Suddenly the tree fell. It fell like a thunderbolt of the gods, killing both girl and medicine man. And instantly their spirits were turned into the white-winged hawk and the lizard, the one ordained to circle the ironbark and the other to cling to its bole till the end of time. And the gods were appeased and sent rain."

Throughout the story the medicine man's eyes never left the children.

The tribe moved restlessly, whispering, like reeds shaken by the wind.

And Sarah covered her face in her hands, appalled. So *that* was why the medicine man had been watching them.

She had understood enough of the story for it to leave her angry and shocked. To her way of thinking she had done nothing wrong, she had simply and in all innocence done her best to look after her brother; but to the Eagle-hawks' way of thinking she had, she now realized, violated a fundamental tenet of the lore. And who was to say which way of thinking was right? There swept over her again the sensation of being divided. You are innocent of sin, the Christian half of her said firmly, but the myall half began to tremble with guilt. She reached for her brother's hand.

"What's wrong?" The boy was close to tears. "Why's everybody staring at us?"

It was the injustice that rankled. If only, she thought, I could explain; if only I could make them understand. She turned to Thoomee. But the lubra averted her eyes.

You too, she thought. She scrambled to her feet. "Come on, Joey." She dragged him out of the circle of firelight, past the arched-up roots of the ficus and away into the desert.

"*Awheeeessh!*" The myalls' sigh faded into the night.

A less civilized people would have killed the children, would have pulled down their tent and left them to die of thirst. But the myalls were gentle, meek as those who one day will inherit the earth; they simply sat and

watched; they made no move to hasten the children's departure; nor a couple of hours later when Sarah and Joey came hesitantly back did they do anything to prevent their return—for vengeance, according to their lights, belonged to the gods and the gods' memories were long.

The children came back because there was nothing else they could do, no other path they could follow that wouldn't have led to certain death. The girl realized this before the camp was out of sight, and it wasn't long before the boy was tugging at her arm. "Sarah!"

"What is it?"

"I want to go back."

"They don't want us."

"But *why?*"

She found it none too easy to explain, and as she expected her brother got only halfway to the truth. "You mean they're angry just 'cause we sleep in the *tent!*"

"Well, that's one of the things they don't like."

"Oh Sarah! Let's go back and sleep with the rest of them. By the fires."

She sat on an outcrop of granite and covered her face with her hands. There was nothing else, she realized, for them to do. But it was a couple of hours before she could pluck up the necessary courage.

She half expected the myalls to drive them away, but the few who were still awake took little notice of the children as they came creeping into the light of the fires. They didn't go into their tent, but curled up by them-

selves on the perimeter of the camp under the roots of a solitary ficus.

The girl didn't sleep at all that night, but lay staring hour after hour at the stars as they crept in slow procession over the ridge of granite: Orion and Canopus, Serpens and Aquila, Scorpio Aquarius and the long-tailed Southern Fish. At first she was angry, angry with the bitterness of one whose Eden turns out to bear poisoned fruit. But in the small hours her anger gradually gave way to sadness. For when she forced herself to think calmly she could see the pity of it: that neither she and Joey nor the myalls were wicked; it was just that they were different, that they didn't understand one another. This, she could see, was their tragedy: that they couldn't communicate, that they couldn't comprehend one another's customs or gods. Yet we've things, she told herself, in common; surely there's some way of bridging the gulf between us? She thought of her friendship with Thoomee. And for a moment the bridge which she longed to discover was within a hairsbreadth of her comprehension. But the moment passed. And by dawn she was conscious only of lips which were swollen and raw, and a too-large tongue gummed up with the roof of her mouth.

Chapter 13

They talked until dawn welled up through the ficus: the leader and the medicine man, searching, probing, racking their brains to find a way of saving the tribe; but they could think of nothing. So they decided it was time to die.

Everything to the Aborigine has its appointed time. There is a time to be weaned, a time to be carried in arms, a time to walk with the tribe and a time to walk alone; there is a time for the proving of manhood, a time for the taking of gins and a time for death—when the spirits decree the time has come it is no use kicking

against the pricks: the one thing there is no time for in the world of the Aborigine is regret. So the Eaglehawks, now, didn't blame their leader for taking them out of tribal territory; they didn't blame the medicine man for his failure to make rain nor the children for provoking the gods. They accepted their lot with equanimity and started to cut their hair and look round for wood and stones out of which to build themselves burial platforms.

But in mid-afternoon, in the hour when the heat of the sun was almost beyond endurance and they had forgotten hope, a rain cloud dark and pendulous came drifting idly out of the north.

The elders went into conference. No good, most of them thought, would come of tracking the cloud; for they were in country which didn't know them and how could they read the signs as to where the cloud would void? But the medicine man wasn't so sure. At the back of his mind was the thought that having already ventured out of tribal territory they might as well go even farther; also he had the intelligence to realize that one cloud might be the forerunner of a front. "It is a message," he said, "from the serpent. We must follow the cloud."

He also suggested that the serpent might look on them with more favour if they punished the breakers of taboo. But the leader shook his head. He lacked his companion's intelligence and powers of clairvoyance, but he had the tolerance that sometimes comes with age and he was fond of children. It was as simple as that. He

couldn't bring himself to believe that the boy and girl who had shyly offered his people a share of their *barramundi* were evil, the evidence notwithstanding. "Let them be," he said. "They are under my care."

So when the tribe set out in the cool of evening to track the cloud—the solitary patch of cumulus becalmed like a ship in irons in the stillness of the sky—Sarah and Joey were allowed to take up their usual places.

Walking by night was more pleasant than by day, for moonlight softened the harshness of the outback and it was mercifully cool. For a while the column picked its way through gibberstones and spinifex in silence; then Sarah floundered into the most difficult conversation of her life. "Thoomee!"

The lubra looked at her inquiringly.

"You and I come from different tribes." She spoke haltingly, conscious that she was using wrong words and uncertain if she was making herself understood.

The lubra nodded.

"And different tribes have different customs, different —oh dear!—totems."

Thoomee nodded again.

"And because we have different customs we have different ideas of right and wrong."

The lubra was puzzled, neither her mind nor her vocabulary being attuned to a discussion on ethics. But when Sarah substituted "good and bad" for "right and wrong" she realized the point that her friend was trying to make. "The lore," she said firmly, "is good. What is against the lore is bad."

"But each tribe has a *different* lore!"

Thoomee's eyes were troubled. "There is one lore," she said, "for us all. And those who break it are lost."

Oh dear, Sarah thought, it's like beating one's head against a wall. She tried another approach. "Joey and I," she said carefully, "are brother and sister, children of the same womb."

Thoomee averted her eyes. This, to her way of thinking, made matters worse.

"And because Joey is smaller than me, I want to look after him: to mother him."

Again Thoomee was puzzled. "You mean you want to love him as a mother loves her child?"

Sarah nodded.

But this was something the lubra couldn't understand; for in myall society children thrive on a love that is communal rather than maternal. "It would be better for your brother," she said, "if he took the love of an *atuakurka*."

"Better to be loved by a boy!"

The lubra nodded, smiling.

And Sarah was shocked into silence.

For a long time they walked without speaking, avoiding each other's eyes, conscious as never before of the width of the gulf that divided them. But round about midnight Sarah noticed that Thoomee's forehead was beaded with sweat and that as she walked her dillybag kept knocking awkwardly against her abdomen. "I'll take your bag," she said.

The lubra shook her head. "Your own is enough."

"Please! For the sake of your baby." She unslung the lubra's dillybag and looped it over her shoulder.

And as their eyes met, the suspicions and fears which they had been plagued by were in a moment sponged away, sublimated as though they had never been by the one small act of kindness.

They carried the bag in turn throughout the night, the one hoisting it onto her shoulder as soon as the other started to flag. They helped each other over boulders and down ravines; they held aside for each other the occasional tangle of scrub; they shared—as much as these could be shared—the rigours of tracking the rain cloud.

The rain cloud drifted this way and that in random currents, now edging toward them, now backing tantalizingly away. They thought for some time that it was thick and heavy with rain, but as they neared it they realized it was thin and anhydrous, little more than a mare's tail hung gossamer under the stars.

They camped dispirited in its shadow in the brief subtropic dawn, and drank their last mouthful of water. Within minutes the very old and the very young were asleep. The others forced themselves to hunt halfheartedly for food, but all they found were a few dozen witchetty grubs in the bark of an acacia.

It didn't seem to matter. For it wasn't hunger from which they would be facing death in forty-eight hours.

The children had no alternative now but to doss down with the others; for they had left their tent by the waterhole. It had been a cruel decision for the girl. We

have done nothing wrong, she had argued, and if we change our habits they'll only think we are ashamed; yet common sense told her that on more counts than one the tent was better forgotten. There was one thing, however, that she had no intention of forgetting. "Joey! Prayers."

Watched by Thoomee, they knelt together in the shelter of the spinifex.

"What are you doing?" The lubra's voice was curious.

"Praying for rain."

"The serpent will never hear you! Without a pole."

"We aren't praying," Sarah said, "to the rain serpent."

"Who to, then?"

"To *our* God: Jesus."

Thoomee was puzzled. "And where does he live?"

Sarah pointed to the sky.

"If he's so far away how can he hear you?"

This, she thought, is getting altogether too complicated. "He can hear us all right," she said. "I know."

"If he hears you, why doesn't he send rain?"

"He will. In His own time."

The lubra was not convinced.

And Sarah had to admit in her heart that she too was beginning to doubt. But she heard herself saying the now familiar words: "Please, God. You helped us before, help us again. Please make it rain. Tomorrow."

And in the early hours of the afternoon an opaqueness came creeping into the sky in the north. Most of the myalls were asleep by the time the opaqueness was visible. But the medicine man saw it. And recognized it. Cirrus. The *tirailleurs* of the front which at long last was moving down from the hills and into the desert.

It was the wind that woke them, the hot dry wind which whipped up the fronds of the spinifex into a *danse macabre*. They had slept all morning and most of the afternoon, motionless as discs of laterite in the lee of a miniature escarpment; but now in the sunset breeze they began to stir. They sat up one by one, ungumming swollen lips and sealed-up eyes and staring first at the spinifex, then at the sky. "*Awhee! Awhee!*" Their exclamations of delight woke the heavier sleepers, and soon the whole tribe were on their feet staring at the sky to the north.

It was dappled with cloud: wisps of cirrus and, farther away and lower, the herringbone patterns of cirrocumulus. Hope, which had been as void as the water in their yallahs, came seeping back.

The appearance of more general cloud was a shot-in-the-arm. But the myalls knew that whole fronts could in the outback be dehydrated and dispersed in hours. They knew too that the very young and the very old were too weak to walk much farther. All they could do was head toward the cloud until they were exhausted. And wait.

So they set off again into the sunset; first the full-grown males, then the lubras, then the uninitiated boys, penultimate the toddlers and gins, and last the medicine man alone. They moved slowly, conserving the last of their strength. They had no energy for foraging for food, though very occasionally a myall would step aside to scoop up a cluster of honey ants or pluck the caterpillars from the leaves of a withered baronia. These titbits weren't a perquisite of the finder, but were thrust into dillybags to be shared round at the next meal.

As the clouds spread, Sarah was filled with elation. It had happened, she told herself, with the pardalote; it had happened with the smoke ring; and now it was happening with the cloud. "I *told* you," she whispered to Thoomee, "our God would send the rain."

The lubra nodded. "But the clouds," she said, "are a long way away. And who knows if they are full of rain?"

They walked into the darkening night.

To start with, the going was easy and the prospect of rain a stimulus; but before long—as the cloud obscured first Aquarius and the Southern Fish and then the skein of the Milky Way—the light became dim and they found it difficult to select and follow a route. By midnight they were exhausted. But the leader walked on. And on and on. And the Eaglehawks had to keep up with him or die.

They kept up.

They kept up, though after the first few hours their limbs ached, their muscles knotted with cramp and their throats grew swollen and raw. Every now and then one of the weaker members of the tribe would stagger and sink to his knees with dizziness or exhaustion; but there was always someone with sufficient strength to help the halt and the lame; and so the column wound on, uncomplaining, locked in the struggle which Aborigines have been waging for twenty thousand years, the struggle to survive.

The clouds to the north, thickening, beckoned them on. But there was not a drop of water now in their

yallahs, and by dawn they had reached the limit of endurance.

The sun was climbing gold out of the gibberplain as they came to a small steep-sided wadi, the headwaters of Sturt Creek. For a moment hope flared up. But for a moment only. For the wadi was full of boulders, silence and little pools of dust. And dry. Dry as the craters of the moon.

They curled up in the shade of the overhanging banks to wait. It was the end of the road. They had neither strength nor inclination to walk another yard. They knew that if it didn't rain within thirty-six hours they would die.

As soon as they stopped walking Joey collapsed face-down in the dust. For a moment he lay still, then his arms and legs started to twitch in unco-ordinated spasms; for he imagined in his delirium that he was back in the Gulf of Van Diemen, swimming. The *ulpmerka* carried him into the shade, and Sarah cradled his head in her lap. She was close to tears. "Don't You *see* what's happening?" she whispered. "And don't You *care?*" She brushed the flies from her brother's face; she watched Ilarra dry-eyed and uncomplaining trying to comfort her baby; she looked first at the myalls, then at the clouds, and still she couldn't bring herself to believe the terrible thing that was happening. "I'd give anything," she whispered, "absolutely *anything*, to make it rain."

Thoomee's eyes were without hope. "Your god," she said, "doesn't hear."

"He does. I know He does."

"Then why doesn't he send rain?"

"I promise you," she whispered, "He will."

The lubra tried to moisten her lips; for the sake of her unborn child she would have prayed to any god, even Wulgaru. "Are you sure you don't need a rain-pole?"

"No."

"Or an offering of blood?"

"Our God," she said, "doesn't ask for that sort of sacrifice." But even as the words formed on her lips she wondered.

The cloud thickened. Thunder rolled muted out of the north. But there was still no rain.

Midday, and the outback dying under a sadic sun: the everlastings crumbling to dust and the parakeelia to powder, rats and ants inert in their holes, and the frogs' skin slack as festoons of net. The myalls lay passive, waiting without complaint for the sort of death that would have driven a white man to delirium. But there were no tears, not even a sigh; for wasn't what was happening the will of the gods? Sarah alone seemed not to have lost altogether the capacity to hope, and in mid-afternoon she climbed to the top of the wadi and stood looking out at the country to the north.

Overhead the cloud was thin, but in the north it was darker and heavier, layer after layer of stratocumulus backed by a wall of thunderheads: and merging into and almost lost among the thunderheads, hills. Were they, she asked herself, the Kimberleys, the longed-for land of her dreaming? At the edge of the wadi a hillock rose

kopjelike out of the plain, and she climbed halfway up it and stood staring at the low, flat-topped escarpment some thirty miles to the north. It was raining, she could see, over the escarpment. But although the clouds had now fanned out into the outback, they lacked (away from the hills) a catalyst to persuade them to void. If only, she thought, we could find a way of making them break.

Dispirited, she slithered back to the wadi. It seemed too cruel: the promised land in sight and the water which could save them only a few hundred feet overhead, and neither within reach.

The sun went down that evening in a contusion of ebony and blood: great thunderheads of cumulus erupting into a crimson sky. But within the hour all trace of crimson had vanished, and the night was as dark as the hole of a rat. It was oppressive and hot; the air was charged with electricity; the myalls had had no water for twenty-four hours, and in the small hours of the night the weaker of them became aware of the presence of Wulgaru, the spirit of death.

First to die was the gin who had dropped behind to comfort the very old man. She was trying to sleep in the shelter of the bank when she felt the nearness of Wulgaru. Not wanting his presence to frighten the children, she crawled a little way up the bed of the river and lay under an overhanging rock. Here, a little before dawn, she died, peacefully and without struggle, dreaming of the days when she had first been bought into the Eaglehawks and of the man who had been gentle as they lay together beneath the acacia.

When Sarah saw the myalls raising the old gin's body onto its platform she covered her face in her hands. There's only one thing, she thought, that can save us now: a miracle. But the clouds that she lifted her eyes to refused to break.

After a while she realized that her friend was sitting at her side. "It's raining, Thoomee," she said, "in the hills."

"But not here."

Silence, cloud scudding low, and thunder muttering like a funereal drum. "How is your baby, Thoomee?"

"He doesn't move." The lubra's voice was matter-of-fact. "I think he is dead."

She was appalled. "He isn't dead," she cried impetuously. "Our God won't let him die. I promise."

Thoomee tried to moisten her lips. "Do you *still* believe in your god?"

"Yes."

"Even though he hasn't sent the rain?"

"Yes," she cried vehemently. "Oh yes, yes, yes." But her vehemence had a touch of hysteria. For what was the use of a God, a voice inside her whispered, who was blind to suffering and deaf to prayer? One might as well pray to Wulgaru.

The lubra came very close to her and stared into her eyes. "Oh Thara," she whispered, "if the medicine man asks you to go with him into the desert to look for honey, don't."

Chapter 14

She lay on her back, watching the clouds as they streamed in a great grey torrent across the sky. Her body was limp as a rag doll, but her mind was clear. It would be an oversimplification to say that she was beginning to doubt; rather she found herself starting to question things which she had taken up to now for granted. This business of being divided, for example, torn almost physically in half between the myall way of life and the Christian: she had been very sure in the past that the Christian half of her was good and the myall half was bad—something to be ashamed of and fought

against. But she began to wonder now if this was altogether true. Wasn't it possible that the two ways of life were complementary rather than antipathetic?

She tried to view the two halves of herself objectively: the civilized Christian at prayer on the steps of the altar, and the Aborigine splayed naked in front of the rain-pole. And it came to her that although the outward appearance of the two girls was different, their thoughts were much the same.

Oh God, please make the clouds break and the rain fall. *Wulgaru, run quickly and tell the serpent to wake.* I've prayed and prayed. What more can a girl hope to do? *Isn't song and bloodletting enough? What more does the serpent want?* I'd give anything, absolutely anything, to make it rain. *And her spirit turned into a hawk and the gods were appeased.*

She shivered. And backward and forward, from light to shade and shade to light, like acrobats on a mad trapeze, the thoughts and the questions she couldn't answer stooped and soared. Until it became more than flesh and blood could endure, and her mind went blank.

It was as though the ticking of a clock in a quiet room had suddenly stopped. Absolute stillness. Absolute quiet. And the sort of peace that passes all understanding. The cloud thickened, but she didn't see. The thunder rolled, but she didn't hear. She lay insentient as clay awaiting the turn of the potter's wheel. And after what seemed like a very long time a still small voice said softly: "Would you really do *anything* to make it

rain?" She nodded. She half expected the voice to go on, but it didn't, and after a while she whispered, "But I don't know what to do."

The thunder seemed to grow louder, and away in the distance lightning stabbed in vipers' tongues of fire among the hills.

Someone was calling her. Calling, calling, calling, from far away and in a tongue that was familiar and yet not wholly understood. "Thara! Thara *Almakeelia*, wake up!"

Her eyes opened unnaturally wide. "What," she whispered, "do you want?"

The medicine man spoke slowly, as though in great pain. "I want you to come with me. Into the desert."

"Why?"

"To look for honey."

She sat up, amazed. This surely couldn't be what God wanted her to do: die in a pagan ritual in the belief that her body would be metamorphosed to a white-winged hawk? "No," she whispered. "No."

The medicine man laid a hand on her shoulder. "Do not be afraid, Thara." His eyes as he quoted the old Aboriginal proverb were understanding. "Death him just like nothing."

She was incredulous: that *he* should be saying this to *her!* "But aren't *you* afraid? Of dying?"

He nodded. "The man who goes walkabout without fear is a fool. Yet the walkabout has to be made."

She stared at him. And as their eyes met she felt for

the first time not fear but a kindredness of spirit. He isn't wicked at all, she thought, only different. I misjudged him because I was afraid of him.

"Come, Thara." His voice was gentle. "It is the lore: that those born of the rain serpent should die for their people."

Maybe I *have* misjudged him, she thought, but that doesn't mean I have to die for his gods. She shook her head.

Thunder rose to a crescendo; and beyond the escarpment at a spot where rain was falling with tropic intensity, lightning struck once, twice, three times at a conical hill.

The lightning fascinated her: flicker and flash and finger of fire astab again and again at the same hill. There must, she thought, be pyrites in it: little veins of iron among the sandstone.

It came to her suddenly what she had to do.

For a moment the risk appalled her. But the still small voice inside her whispered, "You did say you'd do *anything* for rain." And filled with a sudden ecstasy she rose to her feet. "There is no need," she cried, "for us both to die. *My* God has shown me how to make it rain."

He smiled, not for a moment convinced.

She swayed and almost fell, because she was dizzy and faint and the ground on which she was standing seemed to be undulating like the waves of the sea; but her voice had the ring of authority. "Give me your axe."

Wondering, he drew it out from the folds of pandanus.

And she took it into her arms, carefully, as though it were a sacrament. For a moment she stood very still, staring at the little groups of myalls as they lay waiting without complaint for a death that didn't bear thinking of. Then she began to carry the axe to the top of the hillock overlooking the wadi.

The medicine man watched her, intrigued but without hope.

It would be tempting to say that in a moment of revelation she had seen the bridge, the link which was able to unite Christian to myall, Arab to Jew, black to white—the power of love. Tempting but untrue. For she was a frightened child, who saw only the gibberstones sliding out from under her feet and, away on the summit of the hill, a trio of ironbarks framed like sentinels against a backdrop of sky. But one thing she was sure of: no matter what the pain, the risk or the price, she was carrying the axe to the top of the hill. She scrambled up and up, till at last the gibberstones gave way to more solid rock, and she stood panting under the tallest of the trees.

And the place in which she stood took on a sudden familiarity. She had seen it before, in a picture on the wall of the mission: the rocky hill, the desert below, and the three silhouettes etched black against a lowering sky.

She began to tremble. But she didn't drop the axe and run; she laid it carefully at the foot of the tallest of the ironbarks; she fell to her knees and raised her eyes to the cloud.

Thunder and lightning were one. But she neither saw nor heard. For the million volts which leapt from cloud to axe flung her incandescent to the ground. As she fell, lightning struck again and again at the iron of the axehead, thunder pealed out in a wild crescendo, and the clouds shaken by sonic waves trembled and split, and rain in a solid swathe joined earth to sky.

She felt no pain, and in the second before she died she realized that it was raining: raining as though it would never stop, great sheets of water resurrecting plants, animals and Aborigines to life. And the whiteness of the rain grew brighter and brighter until all about her was silence and light.

Chapter 15

It was dawn. Three inches of rain had fallen overnight, and the gibberplain was ablaze with colour: pink parakeelia, violet moola and, most beautiful of all, great multicoloured drifts of everlastings—acre on hundred acre of purple, white and gold. Desert had been metamorphosed to fairyland.

The rain was falling more softly now and the clouds thinning. In their burrows the kangaroo rats stirred, they unplugged the openings and nosed their caches of seed into the moist air; frogs hopped to the nearest puddle and mated in the rain, quickly, knowing instinctively

that the puddles would soon become too shallow for tadpoles to mature in; and after a while a flock of ring-eyed corellas came drifting like a great white avalanche over the plain. The valley of the shadow of death had been transformed to the Elysian fields.

The myalls woke, and the women carried their emu shells to the river and the men went in search of food. The water in Sturt Creek was six feet deep and fast as a millrace, and there was food in almost every crevice among the rocks. By mid-morning hunger and thirst had been assuaged, smoke was coiling up through the rain, and didjeridoo and drum were thudding a jubilate to the gods. Resilient as the flora of the outback, the Eaglehawks had survived, and a way of life old a millennium before the first stone was laid in Babylon went quietly on.

It was midday before a search party of *atua-kurka* found them: the girl and the medicine man together, stretched out between the ironbark. The girl was lying facedown in a pool of water, and the water was over her mouth, and the *atua-kurka* closed her eyes and gashed their bodies with flints to exorcise her spirit. They were afraid at first that the medicine man was also dead, but when they looked at him more closely they saw he was in a trance.

He had been in a trance since dawn.

When thunder burst and rain came cataracting out of the sky, the medicine man had been amazed; for this, according to the lore, was a thing that ought not to have

happened until both he and the lubra were dead. And after a while, wondering, he set out to follow her up the hillock. As he neared the summit, sweat began to form on his forehead and to roll in little salty globules into his eyes; for the scene at the top was macabre as a backdrop to Dante's Inferno. Rain squalls dark as night were scything out of a leaden sky, the tallest of the ironbarks split by lightning was wreathed in smoke, and beneath it the girl was lying facedown in a widening pool of water, dead. He felt sure at first that he must die too to fulfill the lore; and he moved under the still-smoking ironbark and prayed to the serpent to kill him quickly and make an end. He was numb with cold and terror—for the Aborigine as he faces death is buoyed up by no hope of heaven or Valhalla—yet he stood without flinching, hour after hour, waiting for the end which he believed to be predestined. Several times lightning stabbed at the hill —once so close to him that he was flung to the ground and temporarily blinded—but the ironbark under which he was standing was not struck again, and in the small hours the rain began to ease off, and it came to the medicine man in a moment of disbelief that perhaps he wasn't going to die after all. It was soon after this, as the clouds thinned and light came filtering into the east, that he kept on hearing over and over again the voice of the lubra, "*My* God has shown me how to make it rain." And it distressed him almost beyond endurance that he didn't know if the rain had been sent by the serpent or by Another. Maybe, he thought, I misjudged the lubra:

maybe she wasn't wicked after all, only different. And the burden of things that he couldn't begin to understand oppressed him.

It would be tempting to say that as he stood there wondering, he too had a glimpse of the bridge which could span and transcend all differences. Tempting but untrue. For he saw nothing but the thinning cloud and the gathering light and the colours spilling like drifts of ink over a gibberplain restored as by a miracle to life. And as the colours gained slowly in intensity, he willed himself into a trance, hoping desperately that the gods of his ancestors would give him a sign of their powers. But no sign came. And toward midday he realized that the Eaglehawks were milling, purposeless, about him.

They were wondering what to do with the girl: whether to build her a platform or leave her body to the spirits who came by night.

His eyes snapped back into focus. And the first thing he saw was the white-winged hawk hovering high over the skeleton of the ironbark. "Build *Almakeelia* a platform," he cried loudly, "beneath the tree. So that for all time she may come to this place and nest in peace."

And wondering they built the platform, and raised up the body of Sarah Koyama and waited for the medicine man to tell them what to do next.

But he told them nothing; for for the first time in his life the lore provided no answer to the questions he longed to ask. He stood for a moment looking down at the girl. Then, picking up a sharp-edged flint, he gashed his body again and again, great slashing blows

that lacerated his arms and chest until he was covered with blood, and the women moaned and the children rolled up and hid their eyes. Then without a word and looking neither to right nor left, he walked down the hill and out over the gibberplain and on and on through the pink parakeelia and the white and gold everlastings until he was out of sight.

Rain fell softly, and the desert lay silent under a windswept sky.

Chapter 16

"*Arvalla, arvalla!*" The leader could sense the panic
which was threatening to sweep through the tribe. "We
stand," he said slowly, "in country that doesn't know
us, and things are happening that we may not understand. This place is not our place, and tomorrow we head
back for the land of our dreaming." He paused. "The
hawk has gone walkabout, and who knows if or when
he may come back; but we have gained an *ulpmerka*"—
he laid a hand on Joey's shoulder—"and we are alive.
This is the thing that matters. This is the thing that we
have to be thankful for. And remember. That we were

lost and now are found, that we were dying and now are saved." He led his people back to the camp at the edge of the creek.

By night the rain had eased off, the clouds had lifted and broken, and moon and stars shone bright in a cobalt sky. The outback was beautiful by moonlight: silver-grey and as quiet as a deserted church. For a long time nothing moved, but a little after midnight a shadow came edging hesitantly toward the top of the hillock.

It was Joey.

He had set out with high purpose; for it was unthinkable, he told himself, that the body of his sister should be left unburied. But as he neared the place where she lay his courage began to ebb. What, he asked himself, if the evil ones who walked by night were watching; what if Wulgaru himself was lying in wait, there by the blackened stump? As he neared the ironbark, a hawk disturbed brushed past his face with a flip-flap-flip of wings, and he cried out in fear because he didn't know if the hawk was a hawk or the spirit of his sister; and the mystery of things not-understood engulfed him. His fear snowballed. His instinct begged him to run, back to the camp by the creek and the world of drums and didjeridoos whose message he understood. But something held him back—the memory of a love none-the-less deep because he had for so long taken it for granted—and slowly and painfully his resolve hardened, until at last he steeled himself to lower the body of his sister to the ground.

It was more a sarcophagus than a grave that he built

for her, a coffin of stones; and as he worked, he keened; and burial and keening were not incongruous but complementary. He keened softly, the tears running warm and salt over his mouth and down onto the flat, round discs of the gibbers. And when the grave was finished he placed a fragment of ironbark at its foot and walked slowly back to the myalls' camp; back to the world in which he realized (even in the hour of his grief) he would one day be happy: the world of woomera and drum.

The moon dropped under the hills, the Southern Cross rolled onto its side, and the hours before dawn were the coldest of the night. For a while the desert reverted to stillness and a silence so absolute it could almost be heard. Then another shadow, as hesitant as the first, came creeping to the top of the hill.

It was Thoomee.

She was afraid: afraid of the molesters who walked by night; afraid also because it was forty-eight hours since the child in her womb had moved and she felt sure that he was dead and that she would die too. Yet for a reason she couldn't account for she wanted to look again at the face of her friend. As she neared the ironbark the white-winged hawk, disturbed for a second time, flapped angrily into the night, and fear pricked up the hair on Thoomee's neck. But she steeled herself to climb on until she stood looking down at the platform. It was empty.

Her eyes opened as wide as the flowers of a pitcher plant. "Oh Thara," she whispered, "where are you

gone?" She ran her fingers, appalled, over the stones of the sarcophagus: appalled because it seemed to her a terrible thing that the spirit of her friend might be imprisoned there forever in the dark, uncaring earth. Then she noticed the starlight: the gold of the stars reflected and refracted in the gold of the crucifix which had slid from the girl's neck, and lay like a tiny droplet of fire among the flat, round discs of the gibbers. She picked it up. Cautiously. For wasn't this the totem of the God who lived in the sky?

She was running her fingers over the smoothly polished gold when she felt it, faint but unmistakable: the stir of the child in her womb.

For a moment she squatted on her haunches, not daring to believe. Then she felt it again, stronger this time and more persistent: kick, kick, kick. The child who she thought was forever lost had been restored as by a miracle to life.

Her face took on the radiance of sun after rain. For a moment she was too full of joy to think of whys and wherefores. Then the voice of her friend came drifting ghostlike out of the night: "*Our* God will send rain . . . *our* God won't let him die, I promise." And it came to her in a moment of truth from whom the rain and the life of her child had been sent. On impulse she dropped, as she had seen Sarah and Joey drop, to her knees. "Jesus-who-lives-in-the-sky," she whispered, "let the child be a boy."

She saw no vision, she heard no voice, she felt nothing tangible; but as she rose to her feet she felt for a

moment as though she had been standing on the threshold of a great bridge, a bridge that spanned earth and sky and space and time. If someone had said to her, "The bridge is love, the only survival, the only meaning," she wouldn't have understood. She understood only that the child within her was alive and she was happy.

She left the crucifix among the smooth, round discs of the gibbers and pulled up a root from the everlastings which lay in a carpet of white and gold beneath the ironbark and planted it very carefully on Sarah's grave. Then in the gathering brightness of another day, smiling, her hands spread over the child in her womb, she walked back to the camp by Sturt Creek.

Everlastings don't really last forever; but their seed will often take root in unpromising soil, so that great drifts of flowers, unbelievably beautiful, will sometimes spring from the most unlikely plant.

Glossary

BAOBAB

Or bottle tree (*Adansonia digitata*, etc.), described by Saville-Kent as "most extravagantly droll," since its grotesquely swollen trunk contains so much fluid that it is often as broad as it is high. Its gum, mixed with water, makes a refreshing drink.

BANDICOOT

Perameles nasuta: a small ratlike marsupial rodent unique to Australia. Nocturnal and omnivorous in habit, and often covered with ticks—hence the saying "miserable as a bandicoot."

BARRAMUNDI

Scientifically the freshwater fish *Osteoglossum Leich-hardtii*, but widely used as the name of a large tidal perch found in Queensland and the Northern Territory: a fish of fine flavour: features frequently in Aboriginal drawings.

BILLABONG

A section of river, usually a cut-off meander or ana-branch. From *billa* (a river) and *bong* (dead): in New South Wales Aboriginal dialect the name is specifically applied to the Bell River.

BINDIBU

The Bindibu have been described as "a group of unrefined primitives wandering in little bands across the seared red rock of Australia's central desert." (*The Desert:* A. Starker Leopold and The Editors of *Life.*) It has also been said that they are a race of have-nots—"they have no homes, no clothes, no herds and no crops" —what, however, they do have is a stupendous will to survive. Also—again to quote *The Desert*—"they lack neither intelligence nor imagination, and the tapestry of their family life and religious belief is as intricately woven as it is among the most civilized people."

BITTERN

Botaurus poiciloptilus, widely known as the Boomer or Bull-bird because of its call—"three or four deep booms, like the bellowing of a bull." The bittern frequents swamps, and its booming is associated with the bunyip—a mythical river creature with the head of a snake and the body of an ox.

Brigalow

Acacia harpophylla: a small scrublike tree of the *Mimosaceae* family, very resistant to clearing since its branches sucker on contact with earth: hard, perfumed bark and greyblue-to-silver leaves.

Brolga

Or Native Companion (*Grus rubicunda*), the only Australian crane: a tall, stately, long-legged bird, slate grey with a red head-patch. Flocks of brolgas perform bowing, graceful quadrille-like dances. They fly exceptionally high, have a trumpetlike call, and build no nests.

Coral Tree

A tall flowering tree of the genus *Erythrina:* lightweight wood, prickly branches and flame-coloured flowers followed by red-brown pods, sometimes poisonous.

Corroboree

From the Botany Bay *corro* (to dance) and *boree* (sacred ground). Whites apply the term to any Aboriginal gathering from a campfire singsong to a deeply religious ceremony involving song-cycles and dancing.

Didjeridoo

The drone-tube of north Australia: an Aboriginal musical instrument consisting of a hollow piece of bamboo usually about 4½′ long. It is blown trumpetwise, cheeks puffed out to sustain the note which resembles an organ bass. Didjeridoos are usually two-thirds plain wood and one-third painted in narrow rings of red and black. Before playing, the musician will pour water down the tube to improve its tone.

DINGO

Canis familiaris antarcticus: the only indigenous Australian land mammal that is carnivorous: a sandy-coloured native dog which hunts in all parts of the continent except where it has been exterminated as a killer of sheep. Domesticated by Aboriginals as a camp dog.

DREAMING

It needs a book rather than a glossary note to distill even the essence of an Aboriginal's dreaming or spiritual life. But two sayings epitomize his lore: "By faith we live, by force we perish" and "He who loses his dreaming [i.e. his faith] is lost."

EMU

From the Portuguese *ema* (a large bird). *Dromaius novae hollandiae:* the largest Australian bird, and the largest of all birds in the world except the ostrich, it stands about 5' high and is strong-running and flightless. Lives in semi-desert but needs a modicum of green foliage. An emu and a kangaroo are "supporters" in the Australian coat of arms.

EVERLASTINGS

Helichrysum semipapposum: drought-resistant white, yellow, mauve or pink clustered flowers about 18" to 2' high. After rain they form great carpets of rich colour.

FICUS

The Australian fig (*Ficus macrophylla*): a large spreading tree growing up to 150' in height: smooth, latex-impregnated bark, glossy leaves and inch-long figs, the *desideratum* of the flying fox. Remarkable for its arched

roots which lift well clear of the ground like flying buttresses.

Flying Fox

Or Giant Fruit Bat (*genus Pteropus*, etc.): lives in and feeds on ficus or eucalyptus, but sometimes damages orchards of soft fruit. Feeding crepuscular and nocturnal. Next to man flying foxes have the most highly organized auditory and nervous system.

Goanna

Monitor lizard (*Varanus gouldi, V. varius*, etc.): There are more than fifteen varieties, ranging from rock lizards of 9″ to tree-climbing monitors of 7′. All have long, forked tongues, strong claws and formidable serrated tails. "Goanna" began as a corruption of iguana, but is now accepted as an indigenous name, not a misnomer.

Gum

The widely used name for eucalyptus, a genus containing more than 500 species which among them cover 90 percent of the forested area of Australia. They range from the 300-foot mountain ash (*Eucalyptus regnans*) to the one-foot prostrate malle (*Eucalyptus dumosa*).

Humble Bush

Or panic grass (*Panicum*): a tufted perennial form of vegetation with small feathery heads which are easily blown off by wind or vibration.

Ironbark

A genus of eucalyptus having a hard, grey, gum-yielding and deeply fissured bark; the timber is exception-

ally hard and is often used by Aboriginals for spears, shields, boomerangs, etc.

JABIRU

The black-necked stork or policeman bird (*Xenorhynchus asiaticus*). A 4′ black-and-white bird with red legs, becoming rare. Frequents swamps and lakes in the Northern Territory, where it is often seen striding along and stabbing at fish with its huge bill.

JACANA

Irediparra gallinacea: A shy, light, long-legged bird sometimes called the lily-trotter or Jesus-bird "because it can often be seen apparently walking over the surface of the water—but in fact stepping on the broad underwater leaves of the water-lily."

KOOKABURRA

Best-known Australian bird, the world's largest kingfisher (*Dacelo giges*), called by early Europeans the Laughing Jackass because its call is like sardonic human laughter.

KURRAJONG

Brachychiton populneum: a graceful tree growing to about 60′, with oval lobed leaves and green-to-white flowers rich in nectar. The young shoots are often eaten by cattle and used by Aborigines to make dillybags.

LANTANA

An odorous shrub of the *Verbenaceae* family, with varicoloured foliage and small black fruit. It tends to choke out other vegetation (hence its "age-old rivalry" with the suckering brigalow), and in land used for pasture it frequently has to be controlled by hormone sprays.

MEDICINE MAN

Aboriginal medicine men have been described as charlatans and humbugs, but this is a very superficial judgement. The leading authority on the subject is A. P. Elkin, Professor of Anthropology at the University of Sydney, and his opinion is not to be set aside lightly— "Aboriginal medicine-men . . . are men of high degree, that is, men who have taken a degree in the secret life beyond that taken by most adult males. They are men of respected and often of outstanding personality . . . the psychological health of the group largely depending on faith in their powers." Elkin also quotes a number of recorded incidents which indicate the medicine man's powers of telepathy and clairvoyance.

MULGAWOOD

Aboriginal name for a long narrow shield, and hence for the wood out of which it is made: *Acacia pendula*, a scrubby, low-growing wattle, exceptionally close-grained and widespread in dry soil.

MYALL

A "wild" Aboriginal, living tribally away from white settlement. Originally the Botany Bay tribe's word for *stranger*. Alternative meaning, "a weeping willow."

NALOONGA

Aboriginal name for a species of teal (*Anas gibberifrons*) which congregates in large numbers in streams and swamps in the Northern Territory.

NARDOO CAKES

Cakes made by grinding up into paste and then baking the hard pealike fruit of the nardoo or clover-fern (*Marsilea quadrifolia*).

PANDANUS

Tropical palmlike tree, also known as the Screw Pine from the likeness of its fruit cones to a thin pineapple; it has stilt roots and angular branches carrying tufts of long, narrow leaves.

PARAKEELIA

Aboriginal name for *Calendrinia balonensis*, a fleshy desert herb, useful because of its food and moisture content: small and bright-red flowers.

PARDALOTE

The red-brown (*Pardalotus rubricatus*) and the yellow-tailed (*Pardalotus xanthopygus*) both frequent semi-desert and mallee-scrub. Marked like a leopard, their cry is "a mournful ventriloquial whistle repeated four or five times in quick succession."

RAINBOW SERPENT

The rainbow serpent (*Yurlunggur* to the Bindibu) moves through the myths of all the tribes of Australia, and is nearer to godhead than any other creature. The great snake is said to have appeared in the Dreamtime, the time of creation, to have fashioned the earth and then gone to ground east of the Kimberleys at a place where the rainbow plunges from earth to sky. Rain, according to some tribes, is the serpent spitting; and when the rainbow appears they say *Kaio Kuriaio* (no more rain).

SMOKE RINGS

The idea of smoke rings giving complex messages is a myth. All most of them say is "Someone is here and is making his presence known," and the only reason for

breaking up the smoke column is to distinguish it from a bush or cooking fire. Some tribes, however, will send up answering rings as a sign that the approaching strangers are welcome.

Spinifex

Or porcupine grass: a hummocky grass with thin quill-like leaves and seeds carried on an elastic spine. There are many species, of which inland *triodia* and *Pletrachne schinzii* are the most common.

String-bark

A genus of eucalyptus (*E. macrorrhyncha, baxteri, scabra, globoiden*, etc.), the bark of which peels off in long fibrous strips.

Tamarisk

(Genus *Tamarix*): a heatherlike shrub which grows on poor calcareous soil and is tolerant of a wide temperature range. It has thin, spidery branches 2′ to 3′ long with small scalelike leaves and tiny pale pink flowers.

Tuatara

Common name of the aberrant lizard *Sphenodon*, sole survivor of a reptilian line older than the dinosaurs. A dark olive-green in colour with white speckles on its sides and yellow spines, the tuatara is reputed to be the least mobile creature on earth.

Tulipwood

Or cabinet-tree, so called because of its hard close-grained wood. *Harpullia pendula:* a graceful 80′ tree with yellow flowers, red-cum-yellow fruit and spectacular masses of berries.

There are more than five hundred Aboriginal tribes in Australia, each with its own language, customs and beliefs. Of these tribes the Bindibu are the least known, "a people so isolated among the secret waterholes of the desert that they have been seen by only a handful of white men." My portrait of them and the land they live in is as accurate as it is possible to make it; but some details, inevitably, are based on conjecture.